It went on like t̶h̶̶a̶t̶. Quent would go out with me, one time with Eve. It was fun and we knew he was surprised at our lack of jealousy, which made it even more fun.

The first time he kissed me, I told Eve.

And the first time he kissed Eve, she told me.

At a party one night Quent said to the both of us, "You girls are very unusual. I mean, I like you both, but it just seems strange to me that you *don't* mind."

Eve laughed. "Would you like it better if we fought over you?"

Quent looked startled. "Of course not. I know you're best friends. I wouldn't want to make trouble between you. It sure makes it nice for me, but. . . ."

**Other Apple Paperbacks
you will enjoy:**

# I THOUGHT YOU WERE MY BEST FRIEND

## Ann Reit

AN
**APPLE**
PAPERBACK

SCHOLASTIC INC.
New York Toronto London Auckland Sydney

ISBN 0-590-44618-5

12 11 10 9 8 7 6 5 4 3 2 1          0 1 2 3 4 5/9

Printed in the U.S.A.                    01

First Scholastic printing, October 1988

*For Midge*

# Chapter 1

I watched Eve sitting on her bed, her knees drawn up to her chest, and her head bent toward her feet. She was carefully painting small white dots on top of the bright purple polish already on her toes. The tip of her tongue was sticking out of her mouth and she was barely breathing. Suddenly, she let a huge, noisy burst of air out of the corner of her mouth, trying to move a dark brown curl of hair away from her eyes. That was like Eve. She could do a totally graceless thing and look good doing it.

"Eve," I said softly, so as not to startle her and spoil the little white dots, "why are you going to all that trouble to put polka dots on your toenails, where no one will see them?"

"Right," she breathed. "No one, *including* my mother."

"Good thinking," I agreed. "She wouldn't

like it. Now, *my* mother wouldn't notice it if I painted dots on my *face*."

Eve stopped painting her toes and looked at me. "That's not true, Phoebe. She notices a lot more than you think." Eve reached over and brushed a speck of white paint out of my hair.

I wished my hair were like Eve's, wild and dark and curling madly around my head, but mine was blonde and straight and long. I wished my eyes were dark, dark brown and big like Eve's, but mine were blue and not very interesting.

I thought about what Eve had said and then shook my head. "You're wrong. She doesn't notice. She's always too busy fighting with my father. Fight. Fight. Fight."

"War. War. War," Eve said and grinned. "I'm sure he comes back."

"What does *that* mean?" I asked patiently. Eve was like that. She often left whole sentences out of her conversation. She *thought* she said them. In her head she had, but in reality she hadn't. Listening to Eve was like doing a jigsaw puzzle. You had to fill in the blank places. Her brain seemed to move faster than the words would come out. It made being her best friend more interesting than being with a girl who talked in real paragraphs. I was used to it and could usually follow her, but this time I had to ask, "*Who* came back?"

Eve closed the bottle of polish and waved her hand back and forth over her toes to dry them. "Rhett Butler, dummy. I think he comes back to Scarlett O'Hara. Scarlett is the one who said, 'War. War. War.' "

"No, she didn't," I said firmly. "She said, 'If you say "war" just once more, I'll go in the house and shut the door.' She said it to the Tarleton twins and I don't think Rhett comes back at all."

Eve and I had each read *Gone With the Wind* four times. We read it aloud sometimes and acted out the parts, drawing lots for who would be Scarlett. Though Eve didn't really care what part she got, she threw herself into them all, even Aunt Pittypat. Eve would say each word as dramatically as she could, waving her arms as she spoke. We had seen the movie twice in a real theater, and once on television. We were experts on almost every word in the book.

"Well," Eve said, "she certainly notices when you're late for dinner."

I knew Eve was back to my mother. "Maybe I exaggerated. She'd notice, I guess, if I ran away from home, especially when it was time to put the garbage out."

"Or wash the bathrooms," Eve said.

"Or empty the dishwasher," I added.

"Or feed the dog," Eve laughed. "If you had a dog."

We were like that. We could easily add to each other's thoughts. We often ended up lying on the floor laughing hysterically, not knowing what we were laughing at.

Now Eve stood up and gazed at herself in the mirror. "I know it," she said. "I just know it. I am *not* my mother's child. I was stolen from the gypsies as an infant and raised in this totally middle-class family."

I laughed and watched Eve brush her tangle of dark hair. "Gypsies," I said with disbelief. "You look just like your mother, Eve. You're no gypsy."

Eve swung around. "How do you know? How do you know for sure? I could be a gypsy princess, with a whole band of loyal subjects waiting for my return to lead them around the world. To Tahiti, and Paris, and Iceland."

I snorted loudly. "Gypsies in Iceland? Eve, you're nuts sometimes."

"Ha!" Eve shouted and grabbed my hand. She peered intently at my palm, tracing the lines with a finger. "I see," she whispered in an accent that sounded like a combination of a vampire and a U.N. interpreter. "Your name . . . it is Phe . . . Phe . . . Phoebe . . . Phoebe Hadman. You have par-

ents you think fight all the time . . . and no
brother . . . no sister. Lucky Phoebe. I see a
small oven. It is open. . . ."

"There's nothing cooking in it, I can tell
you that," I said.

Eve ignored me and continued. "I see
pots. Lots of pots. *Aha*. Pottery. Your
mother, she is a potter; she is making a
bowl."

"That no one will buy," I added.

"Phoebe," Eve said menacingly. "I see a
man . . . your father . . . he is with people
. . . helping them . . . aha — he is a social
worker. Ah . . . wait . . . you have a friend
. . . a best friend . . . Eve . . . yes, Eve . . .
Eve Patterson. Again, how lucky you are.
What a wonderful girl Eve is."

I giggled loudly and tried to pull my hand
away, but Eve hung on tightly. She closed
her eyes and swayed back and forth. "I see
you have had many summers . . . many."

"An Indian gypsy," I muttered and Eve
said, "Shut up."

"Many summers," she continued. "Fourteen of them, like your wonderful friend
Eve. Aha!" Now she really shouted. "I see
a prince, I do. A prince coming to whisk you
away on his Honda."

Now I leaned forward and stared into my
palm, too. "Where? Where is the prince on
the Honda?"

Eve pointed to a spot on my palm. "There! You see? Purple . . . for royalty."

"That is your purple nail polish," I said with disgust. 'That is *not* a prince!" I pulled my hand away and threw myself across Eve's bed.

Eve looked at me and put a dab of white polish on my cheek. "You are such a realist, Pheb. How did we ever get to be best friends? I remember the first time I saw you. A scared rabbit of a little girl who came into the second grade class and practically sank through the seat. A real little rabbit."

"I was *not* a scared rabbit," I said defiantly. "I was mysterious. That's all."

Eve grinned that Eve grin. The one that lit up the room, the house, the world. "Okay, a mysterious scared rabbit."

Now I grabbed Eve's hand. I pulled my hair over one eye and let it fall over my face as I gazed into her palm. "I see a crazy girl who thinks she's a gypsy, when really she has lived her whole life in Owentown, PA. I see two parents who never fight. Lucky Eve. I see film. Lots of film . . . a theater. A movie theater. Your mother and father are there. They own a movie theater. Oh . . . wait. I see a sister. She has sixteen winters. Every one with a different boyfriend. Lucky sister Heather."

Eve took her hand away and sat cross-legged on her bed. "How does she do it? Heather, I mean. How come she always has a boyfriend, when she's so mean and dumb?"

"She gives off the right vibes. That's what all the magazines say you have to do. To get a boy, you have to let him know you're interested. And anyway she isn't mean and she isn't dumb. She's beautiful and quite pleasant."

"*Pleasant*," Eve repeated. "What kind of word is that to use about a human-type person? Pleasant is for the weather or stewed chicken. Anyway, *she* was pleasant and only got Ashley, not Rhett Butler. The pleasant people get the Ashleys, the Scarletts get the Rhetts."

I knew. I knew the "she" was Melanie, back to *Gone With the Wind*. "Melanie," I said, "was brave and loyal and kind."

"And bor — ing," Eve finished.

"Eve," I said as I picked my coat up off the floor and started to put it on, "you think everyone who isn't bizarre is boring."

"Who? Who?" Eve asked, flinging her arms above her head.

"Well . . . Ernie Farber, for one. He's a perfectly nice boy that you are really mean to."

"Ernie Farber? Ernie Farber is the pits. He barely speaks."

"He's shy, Eve. And he has a crush on you."

Eve looked interested now. "He does? How do you know?"

As I gathered up my books, I smiled mysteriously. "I don't have to tell you how I know. I just know."

"Phoebe! Best friends don't keep things that are crucial to existence from each other."

I walked to the door of her room and said, "Because I heard him telling Chuck Bernstein."

"Chuck Bernstein barely speaks, too. What were you doing, hiding in the boys' room?"

I laughed and pushed Eve's hand off my arm. "I was sitting in front of them on the bus. I was all scrunched down in my seat and they didn't see me."

"Well," Eve said, "Ernie might be nonverbal but he obviously has good taste." A self-satisfied look settled on Eve's face.

"Nonverbal? Where did you get that from?"

"From a book Heather has. It's called *How to Communicate with the Opposite Sex in Nonverbal Ways.*"

"*Good-bye*, Eve. I have to go home," I said, trying to think of one nonverbal way my mother would let me do.

Eve grabbed my arm again, "Stay for dinner. My parents are going to be at the theater late and it's just me and Miss Pain in the Neck."

I pushed Eve's arm away again. "Eve, let go! My mother is expecting me."

We walked down the stairs from Eve's bedroom and I took a deep breath. The Patterson's house had a very particular smell. Heather's perfume, which had some man's name. Mr. Patterson's pipe tobacco, which also had some man's name. And popcorn. Because Heather was always bringing gigantic tubs home from the movie theater. *My* house always smelled of wet clay and cinnamon. The cinnamon because my mother had spilled a huge can of it in the grocery closet a year before. It had fallen into the cracks on the shelf and hours of scrubbing had never gotten it all up. With my eyes closed I'd know if I was in my house or the Pattersons' house. Places have their own smells. Like the school gym, and banks, and old houses.

As Eve and I got to her front door, she said, "At least come in the kitchen and have a Coke, while I start dinner."

I looked at my watch and figured I had ten minutes. "Okay, but just ten minutes. No more."

"All right! All right," Eve said petulantly.

"What makes you think I even want you around more than that? Unless you know some other boys who have crushes on me."

Heather was in the kitchen, sitting on a chair with her feet up on the table, reading a history textbook.

Eve grunted, walked over to the table, and pushed Heather's feet to the floor. "Of all the disgusting things, Heather. Putting your *feet* on the kitchen table is the most. We are going to *eat* off that surface and you have just contaminated it. Wash it off! Good!"

Heather just stared at Eve and shook her head in disbelief. "Cool it, will you? Don't get hysterical. I haven't been walking in a stable, you know."

But Heather got a sponge and casually wiped the table. I realized for the first time that Heather looked like me. Her hair was long and blonde and fell around her ivory face. Her eyes were almost green and she was tall and very slim. Heather and I could have been sisters.

Heather smiled at me and said, "Stay for dinner, Pheb. I don't want to be alone with Godzilla here."

I smiled, shyly. Heather did that to me, made me feel shy. Maybe it was because I admired her. "I can't. My mom said be home by six."

Heather shrugged and walked over to me. She took the tail of the pale blue man's shirt she wore hanging over her jeans, and wet the tip of it with her tongue. Then she scrubbed at the white polish Eve had put on my cheek. The shirt smelled like peppermint, from the gum Heather was chewing. I stood very still, feeling connected to her. I would never tell Eve, not for anything, how I felt about Heather . . . that I wished she were *my* sister. Wished it a lot. It wasn't that Heather paid that much attention to me, but she didn't treat me like her kid sister's pesky friend, either. She was always gentle with me and made me feel . . . worthy.

When Heather dropped her hand from my face, I smiled at her and she grinned, somewhat like Eve but not. Eve's smile was like soda, with popping bubbles and fizz; Heather's was like cream.

I picked up my books again and called over my shoulder to Eve as I left, "See you tomorrow."

Eve called back, "Talk to you later."

# Chapter 2

As I walked home, I turned up the collar of my jacket against a strong October wind. The streets were quiet and piled with orange and red and gold leaves. I kicked through them, crunching them as I walked. And I thought about the first day I had ever seen Eve Patterson, the day Eve said I was a scared rabbit.

We had just moved to Owentown and it was the middle of the term. What could be worse for a new kid in town than to have to start school in the middle of a year? Nothing! Going to school the first day, I sat in the car next to my mother as she drove through the icy streets. I can still feel the dryness of my mouth and the wetness of my palms and the tears so close to rolling down my face. I clutched my green lunch box and when I saw the handle was wet with my perspiration I put the box on the floor of the car. I stared straight ahead and clasped my hands together. My mother glanced at me and said firmly, "You keep your head high and you smile a lot. Smiles are good."

When we got to school, she leaned over, kissed my cheek, and pushed me toward the car door. "I think it's best if you go in alone. It looks better for the other kids. You know where the administrator's office is. We were there yesterday. First door to the right when you go in."

I hesitated and leaned toward my mother. "Go on, Pheb. The first day is only once."

I didn't know what she was talking about, but I went into the school. The principal's assistant took me to my second grade classroom, and the thirty pairs of eyes that followed me to the seat the teacher gave me made me think I would throw up, right there, right then.

The morning was a haze to me, of faces I hated and unfamiliar voices. The chalk didn't even smell familiar. At lunchtime, we were all led to the cafeteria and I was given a seat at a table with six other girls. It was then with a heartbreaking, thumping feeling I realized I had left my lunch box in the car. Everyone was busy opening their boxes and unwrapping sandwiches and I had nothing to eat. I sat with my hands tight together in my lap and gazed down at the table in front of me. Silent. One of the lunch monitors came over and asked, "Did you forget to bring your lunch?"

I shook my head no. I couldn't, wouldn't, admit that I had been so stupid, such a baby, as to leave my lunch somewhere. "I'm not hungry," I whispered.

I ached for the green lunch box and the sliced egg sandwich inside. I didn't want the food; I couldn't have eaten anyway, I thought. But I wanted the box my mother had touched, the sandwich she had made. I wanted my mother, and the egg sandwich was the next best thing. Then I saw a small hand pushing something in front of me. A white paper napkin inched toward me and on it was half of a tuna fish sandwich and an Oreo cookie. I stared down at it and then turned to see who was on the end of the hand. It was Eve. She didn't say a word, just smiled the Eve smile. I looked at the sandwich and then back at Eve's face. Silently, I picked up the sandwich and took a bite. I didn't even like tuna, but I liked it that day. And since then, sometimes when I'm feeling scared or lonely, I eat a tuna sandwich. I know that sounds corny.

That was the beginning.

After lunch, as we left the cafeteria, Eve took my hand and led me back to the classroom. She was my friend. I knew it.

Scared rabbit, she had just said. I'm still scared of things. Not forgetting my lunch, but mostly scared of my father. Not of him as a person, but that he would one day just pack up and leave. They fight so much, my mom and dad. Why wouldn't he leave? Funny, I don't think my mother would go. After all, she's Mom.

As I walked into my house, I smelled the wet clay. "I'm home," I yelled.

My mother answered dreamily, "I'm in the studio. Come see something wonderful."

I walked into my mother's studio, which was filled with bowls and ashtrays and unidentifiable pieces of sculpture. She was lovingly running her hand over a bowl she had just made.

"Look at it, Phoebe. Isn't it beautiful?"

I looked. "Ma, it seems just like all the others." I gestured toward the rest of the room.

"No! No, Pheb, it isn't. Look at the colors. The way the rust and brown and gold all run together. Feel how smooth it is. It's the best I've done."

Obediently I ran my hand over the bowl. It did feel nice, smooth, like satin. "It's nice, Ma."

She shrugged. "I almost sold one today. Mrs. Farber was here and said she'd be back after she thinks about it a little more."

That will be the day, I thought. "What's for dinner, Mom?" I asked, changing the subject.

"Dinner?" she asked with surprise.

"You know, Mom. The thing people eat at the end of the day?"

"Oh, Pheb. I *meant* to go to the market and the day just got away from me."

I turned away from her, feeling rage. I wanted to scream and cry. "What about Dad? He'll be furious when he gets home and finds out you don't have anything to eat. Ma, why can't you remember things like that?"

Betty Hadman took her hand away from the potter's wheel and wiped it on her jeans. "Your father is working late tonight, and I don't know why I don't remember things like that."

She looked out of the window at the tree branches banging against the side of the house. I had to admit she was pretty. Her hair was blonde, like mine, but darker. It was carelessly pinned to the top of her head and golden pieces curled around her face and down the back of her neck. Her eyes were brown. Strange, blonde hair and brown eyes. She was tall like me, and so slim that she looked like she would break if she bent over. But she was strong. I knew that whenever I saw her wrestling with a huge tub of clay.

"Come on," she said. "I'll fix us something to eat." She pulled me toward the kitchen as she spoke.

"I thought you said you didn't have anything."

She continued pulling me with her. "I don't have anything planned. I don't have a *Family Circle*-type meal: chicken, steak, stew. But the cupboard isn't bare, you know."

In the kitchen, which still had the breakfast dishes on the table, she opened the door of the grocery closet. Cinnamon filled the room. "You know, I'm beginning to like it," she said. "The smell, I mean. It's homey."

"Dad says it smells like a cheap bakery."

"Your father has no poetry in his soul," my mother answered, as she opened a can of tomato soup.

As I had to admit my mother was pretty, I had to admit she could take nothing and make a pretty good dinner out of it. It was just a bowl of tomato soup but there was a dollop of sour cream floating on top. It was just melted cheese sandwiches, but it wasn't plain old American cheese, it was something she called Jarlsberg. Of course, she had to cut the mold away before she could use it, but it was still good. Red flecks of paprika covered the top of the cheese. For dessert she halved two pears and drizzled chocolate sauce over them and she made a strong, flowery-tasting tea.

She looked at me, waiting. "Not bad? Right?"

I smiled tentatively. "Not bad."

I pushed my hair off my face and felt the dot of white polish still there. Heather hadn't gotten it off. I looked at my mother and said, "I have polish on my face. Don't you notice?"

She peered closely at me. "You have what, where?"

"Polish," I repeated. "On my face."

She bent so close I could feel her chocolately breath on my cheek. "Oh yeah, now I see it. It's tiny."

I had been right. She hadn't noticed until I pointed it out to her. Here I was, a walking bottle of white polish and she hadn't even noticed.

I went up to my room and felt, as always, how much I liked its neatness and quiet. I was probably the only teenager in the world who never had to be told to clean a room. My mother said she wished I were a slob, so that she didn't have to feel guilty.

I did some homework and when the phone rang at eight I knew it would be Eve.

She didn't stop to say hello, but just began. "It's your turn to pick the colors for Saturday night. What do you want?"

Eve and I had a ritual. When we went to

a party we would wear the same colors in reverse. If I had on a green skirt, and a yellow top, she wore a yellow skirt and a green top. We even bought our clothes so that we could always do that. No one else knew. We took turns choosing the colors. We were going to Carrie Donovan's party on Saturday, and I picked tonight.

"Let me think," I said slowly.

"Please," Eve said, "don't pick something that looks awful on me, like eggplant."

"Or zucchini," I added.

"Or asparagus," she went on. "Although Scarlett made a dress out of the green velvet draperies when she was going to visit Rhett in prison. And she didn't look bad."

"Yeah, but she was going to see Rhett Butler," I said with longing. "What have *we* got?"

"Tomorrow we'll have to go over who we think will be at Carrie's. Then we can decide how to act with them."

"Eve, you know who will be there. No Rhetts, that's for sure."

"Phoebe, maybe we should move. To another place, I mean. Our social life here is just dumb and uninteresting."

I lay back on my bed and stared at the ceiling. "Okay, you talk your parents into selling the theater and settling in New York. And I'll make my parents move, too. . . .

You're nuts, Eve. We have to do the best we can in Owentown."

"Well," Eve said, laughing as she spoke, "there's always Ernie Farber. Okay, so what's it going to be?"

She was talking about colors again. That's what I mean about Eve. "Okay," I said. "I'll wear the gray short skirt, my red sweater, and those printed red tights. Now, you."

Eve thought for a minute. "You picked good, for a change. I'll wear my red pleated skirt, the gray fuzzy sweater, and those crazy gray stockings your mother gave me last Christmas. Listen, I hear my mom coming upstairs to pester me about my English report. Pick me up tomorrow morning."

When we hung up I thought about Ernie Farber. Actually, I liked him, because he didn't scare me. Once in a while he even said a whole sentence to me . . . and I could even say a whole sentence back. Boys just made me uneasy. I knew they were human beings, too, but they seemed so *different* to me.

# Chapter 3

The next morning as Eve and I walked to school, she ran through the boys who would be at Carrie's on Saturday.

"Johnny, Bob, Jeffrey, Ernie, Chuck. Ugh! Not one worth our being our wonderful, charming, brilliant selves for. Okay, I'll take Chuck for the first part of the evening and then you take him for the second. He's the best of the bunch. Don't you think?"

I stopped walking and just stared at Eve. "How do you know he'll want to be with either one of us?"

Eve just kept walking. "Of course he will. He's sensible, isn't he? And we are the most exciting girls in this town." Eve spoke with total assurance.

I kicked at a stone in the street and pulled my jacket tight around me. It was almost cold that morning. "Maybe you are, but not me."

Now Eve stopped walking. "You, Phoebe, are a wonderful human being. You . . . you have *depth*. I'm . . . I'm, well, sort of strawberry icing . . . but *you* are the cake."

She smiled at me, but there was a look on her face I'd never seen before. As if she was scared. It was gone before I could name it, and she was Eve again.

She grabbed my arm and pulled me along. "We're going to be late. Move, Pheb."

Eve and I had a routine for parties. Our fathers would take turns driving us to the party and picking us up, and we would sleep over at the house of whoever was the chauffeur. Tonight it was my father's turn. Eve arrived about a half hour before we had to leave and we put all the final touches on ourselves. Another dab of blusher. Another swipe of eyeliner. Another vigorous brushing. I adjusted her angora sweater on her shoulders. She pulled at my gray skirt to make it hang right.

Finally my father called from downstairs, "Are you girls ever going to be ready?"

"Coming, Mr. Hadman," Eve shouted and pulled me to the stairs.

I stopped at the top and said, "Eve, do you know you spend half of your waking hours pulling at me, or pushing me in some direction?"

"I do?" Eve said with surprise. "Gee, I'm sorry. I don't mean to." Then she tugged at me again. "C'mon."

I had to laugh. You had to laugh at Eve or perish.

When we were inside Carrie Donovan's house, Eve looked around quickly. "Just like I said. No one here worth us."

She spotted Chuck Bernstein and smiled her Eve smile, and he opened his eyes wide, staggered by her sudden interest in him. "I'll see you later," she whispered, "when it's time to change shifts."

I giggled at her audacity and looked around the room. Eve was right, it was just the same old kids. Ernie Farber was standing in a corner by himself, stuffing potato chips into his mouth. I walked over and said briskly, "Hi, Ernie. It's a greaty party, isn't it?"

He swallowed a mouthful of chips, coughed, and lost his breath. I watched him sputtering and turning red with embarrassment as bits of chips fell out of his mouth. Across the room, Eve was watching and rolled her eyes upward. Taking pity on him, I handed him the glass of soda in my hand. He drank gratefully and then coughed some more.

"Thanks, Phoebe," he said pathetically.

"It must have gone down the wrong pipe."

I patted him on the back hard, hoping to stop his final gasps. "It's okay, Ernie. Just breathe deeply and slowly."

As he breathed he looked at Eve, who now was enchanting Chuck. "I hope she didn't see me," he said.

Remembering Eve's rolling eyes, I said with a straight face, "I'm sure she didn't."

Ernie was really sweet and he looked so grateful to have me just standing next to him that I squeezed his hand in just plain sympathy. He looked around the room swiftly and then leaned over and *kissed* me. It was so quick that I barely had time to realize what had happened before he ran away. Like Ernie, I looked around the room, sure that everyone had seen us. But no one was looking at me at all. He could have mugged me and stolen the new earrings I was wearing and people would have just gone on eating and dancing and playing around.

Suddenly, Eve was at my side and I was prepared for a hundred questions from her. But she was whispering in my ear and looking across the room. "Who is *he*?"

I followed her eyes and saw a tall, lanky boy, filling a glass with soda. He had reddish brown hair that curled around his head, and big brown eyes. I had never seen him before in my life and, obviously, neither had Eve.

In a terrifying moment, he was looking right at me. I mean our eyes were *meeting*. Quickly, I looked away and grabbed Eve's arm.

"He saw me looking at him," I said feverishly.

"Are you sure?" she asked. Then, "He's coming over here." She pushed at the mop of curly hair framing her face and reached down to pull up her panty hose.

Then he was standing next to us. Without a minute's hesitation, he said, "I'm Quentin Younger. We just moved to town."

He wasn't stammering or nervous or anything. I just stared at him. I was so impressed by his cool. "Quentin?" I repeated. "That's a . . . nice name."

Now he seemed a little awkward, and I felt I had embarrassed him. "Everyone calls me Quent. My mother really went overboard with the Quentin bit. It's a family name. My mother's maiden name."

"Oh," I said, feeling as if I had been rude . . . or something.

Eve moved slightly behind me and said over my shoulder, "This is Phoebe Hadman." Outgoing, daring Eve Patterson was actually almost hiding behind me.

Quent raised his eyebrows slightly and Eve said in a small voice, "Oh. I'm Eve Patterson. We live here . . . I don't mean *here*

. . . I mean not in this house. . . ."

"She means we live in Owentown," I said.
I mean, somebody had to say something and
Eve was just sputtering.

Then, just as quickly as he had appeared
next to us, he was gone, saying, "I'll see you
around." He walked over to Chuck and the
two of them picked out a tape for the stereo.

We stared after him and Eve said, "I hate
myself." I knew what she meant.

When we got back to my house, my
mother was frantically going through the
linen closet, throwing towels and blankets
out onto the floor. "I thought I had clean
sheets for Eve, but I can't seem to find any."

"It's okay, Mrs. Hadman," Eve said
smoothly. "I can just take one of Pheb's."

We went into my room to try to make up
the extra single bed and I was so embarrassed and angry. "She is just like a child.
Can you *imagine*? No sheets. For a *guest*."

My mother ran into the room then, her
arms full of something silky. "Look what I
found! They were a wedding present. I don't
think we ever used them. She thrust two
pale pink, slinky, wonderful satin sheets into
my arms. "Make up Eve's bed with these."

Eve reached out and ran her hand over
the shining, liquidy surface of the sheets.
"Wow. Like *Dynasty* or *Dallas*."

"How come *she* gets these sheets?" I asked petulantly.

"*She's* the guest," my mother said, and grabbing the sheets from me, she started to make up the extra bed.

"But I live here," I answered, my lower lip sticking out.

"I've noticed," my mother said and continued making up the bed.

"Wait," Eve said. "Why don't we each take one, for the top sheet?"

My mother looked at Eve and at me sticking out a lip, and threw one sheet at me. "Take one regular sheet off your bed and give it to Eve. I only put them on yesterday. And I must say, no one could be cleaner than you."

When we were in bed, stretching out underneath the silky, glossy sheets, we both sighed at the same time. "Did you ever feel anything as wonderful as this?" Eve asked. "Not even Scarlett, when she went to New Orleans on her honeymoon with Rhett, had anything like this, I bet."

Before I could answer, Eve was sitting up in her bed, her arms encircling her drawn-up knees. "I hate myself," she said . . . again.

I waited for her to explain . . . as I knew she would . . . in some way.

"I just crawled behind you, like a stupid *child*, when that Quent person came over. I even squeaked when I talked to him. What little I said."

"You didn't squeak," I said, trying to reassure her. "He was kind of cute. Don't you think?"

Eve thought for a moment. "Yeah, I guess he was. He didn't seem very taken with us. I mean, he just said hello and raced off. Who needs that?"

"You weren't exactly bowling him over with your clever conversation," I said, not knowing why I was defending Quent Younger.

"You're right," Eve mumbled. "I was a dud. You saved the night."

Then I remembered. "Eve," I said softly, "Ernie Farber kissed me."

Eve leaped out of her bed and flung herself on mine. "He what? When?"

I told her just what had happened and she listened with her mouth slightly open. "What was it like?"

I shrugged. "It was like nothing. I mean it could have been a fly that just sat on my mouth for a second and flew away."

Eve laughed and went back to her bed. "He'll probably never talk to you again, he'll be so embarrassed."

We talked for a little longer and then Eve was silent. I heard her quiet breathing and I whispered, "Eve, are you sleeping?"

There was no answer. I fell asleep tangled in the smooth, pale pink satin sheet, happy to have Eve breathing softly near me.

In the morning, I woke up and felt a terrible pain in my head. I coughed harshly and I ached in every muscle. I was sick. I looked over at Eve, who was lying in her bed, staring over at me. Her face was pale and she coughed, too. "I'm sick," she said.

"No, *I'm* sick," I answered. "I feel awful. In fact, I think I may be dying."

Eve sat up with an interested expression on her face. "Can I have your blue sweater? I mean if you're dying, someone has to get it."

I pushed my hair away from my hot forehead and cleared my throat. "You're very selfish, Eve. Some worthy charity should get the sweater."

Eve plumped up her pillow and leaned against it. "You're right, I guess. I am selfish." Then she said thoughtfully, "Give your red sweater to the worthy charity."

That seemed reasonable to me. "Okay, you can have the blue one. Tell my mother after I'm gone."

Eve shook her head. "That's not good enough. We have no witness. People could say I made the whole thing up. You have to write a will, Pheb."

"You're crazy, Eve. What would I say?"

Eve was going through the drawers in my desk, looking for a piece of paper and a pen. "It has to be in pen," she said, as she handed me the stuff.

She sat on the side of my bed and handed me a book to lean on. "Write!" she ordered. "I, Phoebe Hadman, being of sound mind and body — "

"If I was of sound body," I said, "I wouldn't be writing this."

"Okay," Eve answered, wrinkling her forehead. "I, Phoebe Hadman, being of sound mind — "

"If I was of sound mind I wouldn't be writing this, either," I said.

"Come on, Phoebe, just write," Eve said. "I do bequeath my blue sweater to my best friend and constant companion, Eve Patterson."

I put down the pen and looked at Eve. "Where did you get that 'constant companion' from?"

"I don't know. I read it in the paper all the time. So and so was seen with her constant companion. So . . . you're my constant companion, aren't you? It sounds good anyway. Legal."

I carefully wrote what Eve had said and signed it with a flourish, as Mother came into the room carrying a tray with two glasses of orange juice. "We're both sick," I said.

Mother felt my head and then went over and felt Eve's. "You both *are* sick," she said. She handed each of us a glass of juice.

"Is it fresh?" I asked dubiously.

"Fresh from a fresh carton," Mother answered with a straight face. "I just opened it."

Eve giggled, but I was annoyed. I knew Eve liked my mother. "You're funny, Mrs. Hadman," she said.

Mother sat down on the edge of Eve's bed and straightened the blanket. "Why don't you call me Betty and call my husband Walt. And Phoebe could call your mother and father Dara and Frank. Doesn't that make sense to you?"

Eve grinned. "I'd love it. It makes us sort of friends."

I frowned. "I don't want to call Mr. and Mrs. Patterson Dara and Frank. It makes me uncomfortable."

Eve groaned. "Loosen up, Pheb. I think Betty's idea is great."

My mother walked over to me and pushed my hair off my forehead. "If it makes you uncomfortable, Phoebe, then don't do it."

Mom looked at both of us thoughtfully. "It seems to me it is senseless for you to go home, Eve. You might as well both be sick in one house, rather than disrupting two homes. I'll call your mother and see if you can stay here."

Needless to say, Dara Patterson was more than happy to have Eve stay with us. Mrs. Patterson came over a lot in the next three days, but left Eve with us. They were wonderful days, in spite of the fact that we both ached and groaned and coughed. My mother kept coming in with custard that hadn't molded and soup that needed more something and rice pudding that was floating in milk. But the custard was in little brown crocks, and the soup was in her best china, and the rice pudding was filled with bits of apple. She brought us silky bed jackets to wear. They needed ironing, but they felt good.

My father came in at night and I hoped, how I hoped, they wouldn't argue. I couldn't stand it if Eve heard them. Twice, I woke up at night to hear their raised voices, but Eve slept through it all.

After three days, being considered recovered enough to stand up, we were sent back to school. Eve's mother came over and brought her clothes, and as she left I heard her say to my mom, "Betty, you're an angel. You have more patience . . . I would have gone nuts with two sick kids."

Yeah, I thought, but your soup would have been good.

*  *  *

The first day we had English together, and after we sat down I turned to talk to Carrie Donovan, who was behind me. There, across the room, was Quent Younger. Obviously, he was going to be in our class.

"He's here," I whispered to Eve.

Eve frowned. "Who's here?"

"Quent Younger. The guy from Saturday night who you underwhelmed."

Eve grimaced. "Don't remind me."

Quent looked over at us and nodded. I mean really *nodded*, which people don't do much these days.

"He's a clod," Eve said.

I had to laugh. "You are such a wild person. How do you know he's a clod?"

Eve narrowed her eyes and peered at me. "Because he hardly noticed us. That's why."


I knew as soon as we walked into the cafeteria at lunchtime, and Eve saw Quent with a gang of boys, that she was going to do something. All the time we were eating Eve was throwing quick glances in Quent's direction and I could see her devious mind working.

Suddenly, she collected all the garbage on the table, threw it on her tray, and said, "We're through, aren't we? Let's go."

I wiped my mouth on a paper napkin.

"We've only been here fifteen minutes."

Eve stood up and filled her arms with her books and notebooks. "That's fifteen minutes too much in this place. If you want to stay, stay. I have to go."

I was finished eating and I had to see what Eve was up to, because she was definitely up to something. I trailed after her as she wound her way through the tables, until we were finally at the table where Quent was sitting. She stopped and, completely ignoring him, she smiled at Chuck. He smiled back, obviously dazzled. And then Eve opened her arms and the books, the notebooks, two magazines, and a KitKat bar fell next to Quent. One small book hit him on the head, not too hard.

Eve gasped. "I'm sorry," she said, oh so sweetly. "I can get so clumsy sometimes." She knelt down and began awkwardly picking up the books, smiling up at Quent every few seconds and apologizing again. "I hope I didn't hurt you. Maybe I should show you where the infirmary is. I mean, concussions are dangerous and you don't necessarily even know you have one when you have one."

Quent helped her stack up the books and smiled back for every Eve smile he received. He was certainly noticing her now.

But Eve knew when to make an exit, just

like she knew when to make an entrance. "We have to go. We're late." She smiled again at every boy at the table and walked out of the cafeteria.

Outside, we ran to a deserted classroom and collapsed in laughter. "What are we late for?" I asked.

Eve shrugged. "For the plane to London."

"For a fitting on my new evening gown," I added.

"For my beauty parlor appointment to have my hair dyed green," Eve said.

"Well, Quent noticed you, if that's what you wanted, Eve."

Eve slipped into a chair and thought. "I think mostly I wanted to hit him on the head. Boys can be so . . . so *strange*."

# Chapter 4

And they certainly were. That night, Mother, Dad, and I were having dinner. It was even almost a real dinner . . . beef stew; though the potatoes were still hard, and the peas were all squooshed in the stew, but it was served from a big china tureen with a fancy silver ladle. When the phone rang, my father said, "You get it and tell whoever it is we are having dinner."

The call, the whole entire call, took three minutes and when I went back to the table I could barely speak.

"Who was it?" Mother asked.

"I don't believe it," I said. "I do *not* believe it."

"It was Tom Cruise," Mother said. When I didn't answer she asked, "Prince Charles? Sting? The Boss?"

"This boy called me," I sputtered. "A boy from school. His name is Quent Younger."

"Well, that's nice," Mother said. "Is *he* nice?"

"You don't understand," I said, pushing the stew around on my plate. "Eve and I met him together and he called *me*. Quent Younger called me and asked me to go to a movie tomorrow."

My father took a drink of water and smiled. "Well, since it's Friday tomorrow, that's okay."

I shook my head. "You're not listening. He called *me* when he could have called Eve."

"Naturally," my father said. "The boy is obviously smart and has perception."

"Walt," my mother said, "that's a misleading thing to say to Phoebe."

I held my breath as my father answered coolly. "Of course it's not misleading. It's the simple truth."

Mother stood up and began clearing the table. "Walt, boys can be smart and have perception and prefer girls like Eve."

I couldn't have agreed more, but now my father was on his feet, too, piling dishes on top of dishes.

"Walt," my mother said stiffly, "you do *not* know how to clear the table without breaking dishes. Be more careful! Please!"

They were at it. And I didn't want to hear any of it. I went upstairs and threw myself on my bed. I stared at the ceiling that my mother had painted a soft, light blue and then had added clouds to. What would Eve say when I told her Quent Younger had called me? Would she be angry? After all, she was the one who had hit him on the head, not me.

We had arranged to take the bus to school the next day, because it was supposed to rain, which it did. As I waited for the bus to get to Eve's stop, I kept practicing what I would say to her. Guess what, Eve? . . . Eve, know what happened? . . . You'll never believe this, Eve, but. . . .

I watched her climb into the bus, her bright yellow slicker emphasizing her dark hair and dark eyes. As soon as she sat down next to me, I blurted it out. "Quent Younger called last night and asked me to go a movie tonight with him and a few other kids."

Eve blinked. "What are you going to wear?" she asked. "Pheb, it's *tonight*. We hardly have any time to dress you."

Relief swooshed over me. "You don't mind? I mean, that he asked me and. . . ."

"And not me?" Eve finished. "I would have liked him to call me, I guess, but it's not like I really like him or anything. Do you?"

I thought for a minute. Actually, it was the first time I had thought about whether I liked him or not. I'd been so involved with what Eve would think. "I don't even know him," I said. "So how should I know if I *like* him?"

Eve agreed. "Right. That's why I don't mind that he didn't call me. Anyway, Phoebe, take notes. Remember every word he says. So if you're out with him, I'm out with him. Or something."

"What should I wear?" I asked. "What if he holds my hand in the movie and I'm all sweaty?"

"That's easy," Eve said with assurance. "When you see him reaching for your hand, you quickly wipe yours on your jeans or skirt or whatever."

"Or on his sleeve," I giggled.

"Or on the arm of the person sitting next to you," Eve said.

"Or on the back of the neck of the person in front of me," I added. By now we were smothering our loud laughs and hanging onto each other. Then I stopped and whispered, "What if I have to go to the ladies' room?"

"Don't!" Eve said firmly.

"Well, what if I *have* to?" I insisted.

"Then just say you have to call your mother or something."

I sniffed. "That will make me seem very appealing to him. A girl who has to call her mother on a date."

Eve leaned back in her seat and smiled a small, self-satisfied smile. "See, I did make him notice us!"

I laughed out loud. "I think he was afraid to ask you to go to the movies. He probably thought you'd decapitate him, or something."

"What time is he coming?" Eve asked.

"Seven . . . I think."

"Okay, I'll be over at six o'clock and we'll get dressed. After all, it is our first *real* date. Not just a party where you go in a mob."

She arrived at five-thirty, with Heather. "I brought *her* along. She does know a lot about clothes and makeup and stuff . . . and she also happened to drive me over."

Eve threw open my closet door and peered in. "Heather, what do you think of this?" She pulled out a pair of light-blue jeans and a light-blue sweater.

Heather rifled through my clothes and came out of the closet with a pale yellow pair of pants and a yellow blouse. "These. You'll look like a buttercup. Wonderful!"

"Supposing he likes roses?" I asked.

Heather ignored me and was busy combing my hair, pulling the sides up and fastening them on the back of my head. I had to admit it made me look . . . more mature. I felt something funny at my feet and looked down to see Eve putting polish on my toenails. No dots, just pink polish.

"Eve, it's October. He's not going to see my feet," I said.

"You never know. Maybe you'll be in an accident and your shoes and socks will be torn off your feet."

Heather stopped combing my hair. "What a dandy friend you are, Eve. So reassuring."

"I'm a realist. That's all," Eve said, continuing to put on the polish.

I felt like a wooden dummy. Eve and Heather pulled and pushed and combed and brushed and polished. My mother came up and stood at the door.

"I don't think I'm needed," she mumbled softly.

At six forty-five Eve and Heather left. Eve whispered to me, "Have a good time. I'll talk to you at dawn tomorrow."

I waited in my room for the fifteen minutes until Quent came. Alone. Thinking. Why am I going out with this boy I don't know? Who cares about him? I'd rather be with Eve or Carrie. I'd rather be reading or watching TV or sleeping. Is this what growing up is all about? Going out with strangers?

There were six of us who went to a horror

movie at the Pattersons' theater. The movie was scary, but I made sure I didn't grab Quent's hands or put my face in his shoulder, as I would have done if I'd been with Eve. Quent bought us a big tub of popcorn and even asked me if I wanted butter or not. I love butter. But all I could see was it dripping down my chin, and my hands a combination of perspiration and oleo, so I said no. The things a girl does for a boy she doesn't even know. Quent did hold my hand, and I didn't even have time to wipe it on my jeans first. But his hand was kind of sticky, too, so it didn't matter. I just pretended my hand was fine and his was the sweaty one.

After the movie, we all went to a pizza place in the mall. We crowded into a booth that was meant for four, and there was a lot of laughing and hooting and the boys blowing the paper from the straws around.

"Do you like anchovies?" Quent asked.

I hated them, but I waited. "Do you?"

"Do you?" he repeated.

"No."

"Good, I don't either," he said.

It wasn't hard to talk to Quent, because we didn't really have to talk to each other. Six of us all yelled at once, about the movie, about school, about a chemical spill in the local river. Then after two Cokes and two glasses of water, well, it was inevitable.

After thinking about it, I said, "I have to make a phone call."

After doing what ladies do in ladies' rooms, I picked up the phone in the lounge part and dialed Eve's number.

She answered and after I said hi, she yelled, "Where are you?"

"I had to make a phone call," I answered.

"What's he like?" she asked breathlessly.

"He's okay. Nothing special."

Eve sighed. "Nuts. I hoped we had really met someone glorious. Oh well, Scarlett had her dumb Charles Hamilton and Frank Kennedy."

"He's not *dumb*. I just can't tell yet."

"So go back and throw yourself into it more."

"Okay. . . ." I was about to hang up when Eve yelled, "Pheb!"

"What?" I shouted into the receiver that was halfway down from my ear.

"Do you think he's going to kiss you good-night?"

"How do you tell?" I asked.

There was silence. "Wait, I'll ask Heather."

"Eve," I shouted. "I have to go." I hung up and went back to Quent.

He didn't kiss me good-night. He didn't even try, and if it was going to be anything like Ernie Farber's peck I didn't really feel I was missing much.

When I went into my house, my mother was reading in the living room. My dad was already in bed. He works long hours and gets very tired by the end of the week.

My mother looked up from her book and raised her eyebrows. "How was it?"

I shrugged. "It was okay. Nothing breathtaking."

My mother nodded. "Good. I'd hate to have a kid who fell in love with every boy who took her to the movies."

"I've *never* been in love," I said. "Maybe I don't know how."

Mother smiled. "You'll learn. Believe me."

# Chapter 5

On Wednesday, when Eve met me in the cafeteria at lunchtime, she looked funny. "What's wrong?" I asked her.

She smiled strangely and said, "It's Quent. He asked me if I wanted to go roller-skating this afternoon . . . at the rink in Norristown."

"That's awful," I said, frowning.

"I knew you wouldn't like it," Eve said. "I'll tell him I can't go."

Eve sank lower in her seat and whispered at me, "*You* said it was awful, didn't you? You don't want me to date Quent. Right?"

I stared at Eve, not believing what she was saying. "I said it was awful, because *you* are the worst roller-skater in the whole, entire world. You'll be a disgrace."

"Oh, Pheb," Eve said. "I'm so relieved. I thought you were jealous."

"Jealous because you're going roller-skating with Quent? I don't even like him that much. But why did you say you'd go with him, when you're going to be on all fours most of the time?"

Eve grimaced. "I didn't want to admit I couldn't skate. Anyway, Scarlett didn't know how to pick cotton and she did all right."

"*She* was saving a plantation. What are you saving?"

Eve grinned. "My pride, I guess. How could I say, 'Sorry, Quent, but I have reached the old age of fourteen and I can't really skate'?"

"He'll find out fast enough, anyway," I said.

I looked at Eve, and though she was beautiful as always, she had on faded jeans, but faded to almost white, and an old sweater that looked as if three of her could fit into it. "I've seen you look a little better, but you're okay."

"I'm nervous," Eve said. "It's bad enough skating with a girl, but on a sort-of-date it's gruesome."

At four o'clock I had a call from Eve. I could hear music in the background and lots of screaming. "This is worse than we thought it would be," Eve shouted into the phone.

"What's happening?"

"I'm on my rear more than I'm standing up. He keeps skating around and stopping every now and then to ask me how I am."

I thought for a moment about how to handle this situation. "Eve, smile a lot. You're gorgeous when you smile."

Eve sighed so loudly I could hear her over the music. "What good will that do? I'm lying at his feet most of the time."

"Just look up and smile. Do as I say. He'll love it."

"Fat lot you know," Eve said petulantly. "Listen, can you come over tonight?"

"I'll try," I said.

After dinner my mother was delivering a pot she had made to some strange person who had actually bought it. She agreed to drop me at Eve's and pick me up an hour later. Eve's parents were in their den going over the account books from the Hollywood Theater.

Dara Patterson called out when she heard me come into the house. "Phoebe, come in here."

Both Dara and Frank Patterson were sitting on the couch with books spread out around them. She took a pencil out of her mouth and said, "We aren't making as much money as we did last year. Something is wrong, like not enough patrons. What would you pay to see at a movie theater, Phoebe?"

"Horror movies," I said instantly.

Mrs. Patterson grimaced and Mr. Patterson said, "And after that?"

"Molly Ringwald."

Dara Patterson said gently, "Anything someone over twenty-five would like to see, too?"

"I'll have to think about that," I answered, as Eve screamed from upstairs for me to come up, already.

Eve was lying on her bed, looking depressed. Heather was sitting on the floor, going through Eve's jewelry box, looking for earrings she insisted Eve had taken.

Eve rolled over and looked at me. "I was a disaster. A total disaster. I could barely remain upright for more than two minutes."

Heather stopped going through the box. "He probably loved it. Whatever his name is."

Eve sat up and pulled her knees to her chest. "His name is Quent. And why would he love it? He took me along for company and he spent the time skating alone."

Heather shook her head knowingly. "Sure, but it made him feel macho. You know, me Tarzan, you Jane."

Eve reached for her hairbrush and started brushing her short, dark curls. "So if guys like the Tarzan-Jane bit, why are we knocking ourselves out liberating ourselves all over the place?"

Heather shrugged. "Don't ask me, ask Mother."

Eve put down her brush and motioned for me to come over. I perched on the edge of her bed and she started brushing my hair. "Well," she said, "Quent Younger is obviously playing the field. First he takes you out, then me. Then you again, and then probably Carrie or something. He definitely is playing the field," Eve said knowingly.

"Well, so are we," I said firmly.

Eve stopped brushing and poked her face in front of mine so she could see me. "With who?"

"With who what?" I asked.

"With who are we playing the field? We aren't dating anyone."

"Don't be so literal," I said with annoyance.

"Well," Eve said, "Scarlett played the field even when she was married."

I frowned. "What do you mean by that? She didn't date anyone when she was married, not any one of the three times."

Eve thought. "No, but she yearned after Ashley all the time."

"Yearning," I said, "is *not* playing the field."

Heather stood up. "Eve, where did you put my earrings? Try to remember. And you two are crazed with all this Scarlett stuff. The girl is fictional, make-believe, and you talk as if she lived next door."

Eve and I looked at each other and grinned. "Wouldn't that be wonderful?" Eve said dreamily.

While my mother was driving me home I thought about what Heather had said. "Mom, Heather said boys like to feel that they are better than girls. She said they like to be Tarzan and want us to be Jane. Is that so?"

"Some guys like that," my mother said. "Not all."

"Eve wants to know why we're liberating ourselves, if guys aren't going to like us that way?"

My mother stopped for a traffic light and looked over at me. I could see her eyes were thoughtful in the lights from the street. "Why do *you* think we are?"

I shrugged. "I don't know. I guess you can't spend your life lying on the floor just because a guy likes it."

"I beg your pardon?" my mother said.

I explained about Eve's roller-skating afternoon.

Mother laughed and patted my knee. I smelled her perfume as she moved over to me. "Your answer is the best I've heard," she said and kissed my cheek.

# Chapter 6

It went on like that for a month. One time Quent would go out with me, one time with Eve. It was fun and we knew he was surprised at our lack of jealousy, which made it even more fun.

The first time he kissed me, I told Eve.

"What was it like?" she asked.

"Well, better than Ernie Farber, but . . . you know . . . so far I haven't been knocked off my feet."

And the first time he kissed Eve, she told me.

"What was it like?" I asked.

"Not bad. I mean, it didn't make me feel sick to my stomach, but . . . there has to be something more interesting than that in the kissing department."

Heather thought we were unnatural. "Doesn't it bother either one of you the least little bit that this guy is going out with both of you?"

I shook my head. "It's okay with me."

Eve agreed. "Why should it bother me? I'm not in love with him, or almost maybe in love with him."

At a party one night when Eve came with Chuck and I came with Quent, Quent said to the both of us, "You two girls are very unusual. I mean, I like you both and I'm glad you don't mind my going out with both of you, but it just seems strange to me that you *don't* mind."

Eve laughed. "Would you like it better if we fought over you?"

Quent looked startled. "Of course not. I know you're best friends. What kind of a guy do you think I am? I wouldn't want to make trouble between you. I can think it's strange, though. It sure makes it nice for me, but. . . ."

I patted his arm and pulled him toward where the dancing was. "Come on, Quent, don't worry about it. Eve and I are just special. Different."

Eve agreed. "Better than most."

"Don't go overboard, Eve," I said.

Eve grinned and went looking for Chuck.

The music was slow and Quent put his arms around me and we danced. We danced well together. I often feel awkward, all arms and legs and extra wrists and ankles, but when I'm dancing I feel good. Like all my pieces are doing the right things at the right time.

"You're a great dancer, Phoebe. Better than Eve."

One short, small stab of satisfaction went through me. I always felt Eve was so much better at everything.

About a week later, Eve and I were in The Record Place in the mall. We were going through the new releases trying to decide which one to buy, when I looked across the store. Quent was standing with John Minero and they were reading the back of a record cover. The light was hitting Quent's hair in a funny way, making it look all shiny and alive. His head was bent slightly, but I still could see every feature of his face. Something happened. I couldn't take my eyes off him and lovely ripples of warmth went from my head to my toes.

He's so good-looking, I thought. How come I never noticed before?

Eve looked at me and said, "What are you staring at?" Then she followed my eyes. "Oh, Quent is over there."

I didn't answer her. Quent looked up, saw us, and Eve waved at him. He walked over.

"John has to get home. Feel like the three of us having a soda?"

"Okay with me." Eve looked at me questioningly.

"Sure," I said, but I didn't really want to go, not the three of us, and I didn't know why.

We went to a soda-and-pizza place called Open and we each got one slice of pizza and a drink. Eve and Quent yakked about all the things we usually yakked about, but I couldn't think of anything I wanted to say. All I knew was that Quent's fingers around his soda were long, and his nails were clean, and he didn't slurp when he drank his soda, and the pizza cheese didn't drip down his chin. None of those things that made other boys — and girls, too — look so disgusting. How come I had never realized how nice his voice was? Loud enough, but still it didn't burst your eardrums. And his laugh was full and happy.

When we left, he had his bike so he rode off, and Eve and I waited for the bus.

Eve looked at me suspiciously. "Are you okay? You barely said 'boo' at the Open."

"I'm fine," I said quickly. "I just have things on my mind." I thought that sounded private enough so that Eve would leave it alone. But Eve is Eve.

"What have you got on your mind?" she demanded.

I was annoyed and thought frantically. "When Scarlett was trying to save Tara did everyone ask her what was on her mind?"

Eve looked puzzled. "Can't your folks meet their mortgage payments?" She really looked worried.

Now I was indignant. "Of course they can. What a thing to ask!"

"*You* brought it up," Eve said. "You mentioned Scarlett and Tara. You're weird this afternoon, Pheb."

And I *felt* weird.

That night Quent called me. "There's a great new horror movie at the Hollywood Friday night. Want to go?"

He had called me before to make dates, to ask something about school, to just talk a little, but his voice sounded different to me. Full of hidden meanings that I suddenly wanted to be there.

"Sure, I'd love to," I said.

"Great. Pick you up at seven."

I hung up and just stared at the phone for a little while. As if it still had the sudden magic of his voice. When it rang again I knew it would be Eve. And it was.

"You okay?" she asked. "You did seem strange this afternoon."

"Eve, you are *so* persistent," I answered.

"That's one of the bad things about having a best friend who knows everything about you. You can't get away with anything."

I did get away with something that night, though. I didn't tell Eve that Quent had called. It was the first time I had done something like that. I just didn't want to tell her . . . then. I did the next day at lunch and, like always, it didn't matter much to Eve at all.

On Friday night, when we got to the theater I asked Quent, "Who else is coming?" We always went to the movies with a group, actually we always went *everywhere* with a group.

"No one else is coming," Quent answered. "Everyone was either busy, or had seen the movie, or didn't want to see it. Do you mind, just us two?"

"No," I answered quickly. "No, it's fine with me."

It was more than fine and I tried hard to believe that Quent had set it up deliberately, because he wanted to be alone with me. We had gotten used to each other so there was always popcorn dripping with butter, and neither one of us cared if our hands got gooey and our faces smudged. But that night I cared again, and I kept wiping my hands and face on the paper napkins. When we left the movie I took a quick look in the lobby mirror, to be sure I was not disgustingly dripping butter.

We went for a hamburger and I felt ill at ease again. It's one thing to talk to a boy who is just a friend, but what do you say to a boy you *like*? Quent didn't seem to be having any problems at all and he just rattled on. Until he stopped and asked, "You okay, Pheb? You're awfully quiet."

I pulled myself together quickly. "I'm fine." Then I forced myself to be the way I always was with Quent, talkative, relaxed, comfortable. It wasn't easy to do, but I must have done it because he didn't ask again if I was all right or not.

At my door he leaned over and very lightly kissed me. This time, without my knowing I was going to do it, my hand reached up and touched his shoulder. He kissed me again and then he ran down the walk. "See you in school."

On Saturday, Eve and I worked together on a report that was due in science on Monday.

"So, what did you do last night?" Eve asked, as she always did.

None of your business, I thought, and then was embarrassed that I'd even thought it, so I gave her a detailed, blow-by-blow description of the evening. More detail than usual, to make up for my rotten thought.

"Pheb. I'm not interested in every breath you took, just the important facts. What's *with* you?"

What *is* with me? I thought. Love is what is with you, was the answer that popped into my head. Love? Me? With Quent? I was staggered. I ached to tell Eve. After all, the first time a girl falls in love she wants to tell her best friend. But what do you do when that best friend is going out with the boy you're in love with? So I didn't say anything. But it was there, in the room. I was in love.

Quent was going out with Eve the next Saturday and when Jeffrey Turner, spur of the moment, asked a gang over, they came together. I was alone, but lots of kids were alone and came by themselves. I couldn't take my eyes off my best friend and the boy I loved. Eve seemed more extravagant, laughed more, danced more, clowned around more. And Quent seemed to enjoy it. Why couldn't I be more like Eve? Louder, more fun, more interesting. Why couldn't my hair be dark and my eyes big?

Quent danced with me, too. He was the same. Eve was really the same. I was the one who was different.

I should have called Eve on Sunday to go over Jeffrey's party. What everyone was wearing. Who seemed attracted to whom.

Who was a wimp. Who was fascinating. But I didn't. I didn't want to hear Eve's feelings about Quent. And Eve didn't call me. That surprised me. I was sure that before the day was over she'd be on the phone. But she wasn't.

When we met to go to school on Monday, we both rattled on at the same time.

"I meant to call."

"I had so much work to do."

"I started to a million times, and something always stopped me."

We didn't meet each other's eyes, just pushed out garbled sentences.

And then, one afternoon, the next week, when Eve and I were lying on the beds in her room studying, everything fell out of place. Heather was in the room, too, looking for a book she insisted Eve had taken. She was going through Eve's bookshelves when the phone in Eve's room rang. Eve answered, looked over at us, and moved the phone out into the hall. The cord didn't stretch too far, so we could hear everything Eve was saying.

"Hi, Quent? What's up? Sure . . . that sounds great. Maybe I'll even be in control of the skates, instead of them in control of me."

I stared at the cord of the phone and listened unashamedly to Eve. Her words were ordinary. It was the tone of her voice that was different. She sounded soft and dreamy and more than friendly.

When I looked away I met Heather's eyes. They were filled with sympathy. "You like this Quent guy, don't you?"

I nodded.

Heather shook her head knowingly. "So does Eve," she said.

I actually gasped. "That's ridiculous. Eve never told me that."

Heather raised her eyebrows. "Have you told Eve how *you* feel?"

"No. Of course not. How could I? How do you know Eve likes him, too?"

Heather looked superior. "It's obvious. And anyway, she just mentioned it to me the other day."

I sank down onto the soft carpet and put my head in my hands. "What do we do, Heather? I mean, we're best friends."

Heather sat down next to me and looked thoughtful. "All's fair in love, Pheb. The both of you just have to keep going out with the guy."

"It sounds *awful*. So hard to do and still be friends."

"Phoebe, what's so special about this

Quent fellow that two super girls — or one super girl and one just okay girl — like him? Why?"

Liking Quent was still so new to me, I hadn't really tried to figure out *why* I liked him.

I thought carefully about it and then tried to tell Heather. "Well, first of all he's fun to be with. He can be *so* funny. He makes me laugh. And he's smart, yet he doesn't act like a genius. And he thinks I'm smart, too. And, well, he asked me if I like anchovies the first time we went out."

"A real gallant boy," Heather muttered. "Go on."

"And he's good-looking. That shouldn't be important, I know, but it sure is nice. And his fingernails are clean and he never keeps me waiting when we have a date. You want more?"

Heather shook her head no. "That seems a fair amount of reasons to like a guy."

Eve came back into the room then, but she didn't mention the call at all. And I didn't ask. We had a new set of rules obviously, without even discussing it.

# Chapter 7

When you've shared absolutely every-thing with a friend, it is very hard to sud-denly have a whole area of life that isn't shared. Eve and I still talked about every-thing in this world . . . except Quent Younger. Well, we talked about little things connected with him, what movie we saw with him, what we wore on a date, things like that. But never feelings. He could have kissed her a thousand times and I didn't know. And vice versa. It was hard. It made what had been a perfect friendship only semi-perfect.

The only good thing about it was it did force us to find other things to talk about to fill in the gaps. And when we did that, Quent disappeared into the background and we were Eve and Phoebe again.

One afternoon, the week after Heather had told me that Eve liked Quent, too, we were in my room. Cans of Coke were perched precariously on the bed along with a bowl of crisp apples and pretzels. That was my favorite snack, but all three had to be there at the same time.

"Phoebe," Eve said. "It's time we decided what we want to be when we grow up. I mean, a career. We are really retarded in that area."

"Eve, I just don't know. I like lots of things. Why do I have to decide now?"

"What are you going to do in college?" Eve asked. "You should have some idea by then."

I took a drink from a soda can and wiped my mouth. "I have years before college. I'll worry about it in my senior year in high school."

Eve stretched out on my bed. "I've decided," she said firmly.

I looked at Eve suspiciously. "What have you decided?"

Eve sat up and looked at me. "I'm going to be an actress."

"No you won't, Eve. You have to sacrifice and struggle and suffer to be an actress. You don't like to suffer."

Eve jumped up and faced me. "That's not true. I don't mind suffering."

I brushed the pretzel crumbs off the bed and then said, "Okay, but you'd have to live in New York in some tiny apartment with three other girls who also want to be actresses, and there would be roaches and stuff like that. Because you won't have any money."

"Why do there have to be roaches?" Eve asked. "Three other girls are okay, but roaches — "

"I don't know," I said with annoyance. "There are *always* roaches."

Eve was silent. "How about if I'm a director, then?" Eve asked.

"I don't know anything about being a director. But you sure like to direct."

"I'll think about that," Eve said.

We were both relaxed, at ease with each other. "It's nice today, isn't it?" Eve asked softly.

I knew what she meant. "It's nice," I agreed.

That Friday night everybody went bowling. Our gang is not much for bowling, but every now and then when we can't think of anything else to do, someone says, "Let's bowl," and we go.

Eve may be awful on skates, but she is a terrific bowler. When she is standing in front of the lane with the ball in her hand, you have to look at her. She's a combination of strength and grace and know-how. The ball always sails down the alley, knowing where it is supposed to go. It's not always a strike, but Eve's bowling ball never goes into the gutter.

I smiled as I watched her, proud of her. Quent was standing next to me and he was watching Eve, too. I was about to say something like "Isn't she great?" when I realized he wasn't watching what I was watching. It wasn't the bowling ball or Eve's arm drawn back or the way her legs were positioned that Quent was looking at. It was Eve's face. Her eyes filled with excitement and confidence. Her cheeks flushed with a sweet, pale pink and a mist of perspiration on her forehead that just made her look dewy, not sweaty. I knew he saw the way her dark hair curled around her face and head, and how she was biting her lower lip, making her teeth look whiter against the pink of her mouth.

He was just staring at her, and I knew. He liked her. He liked Eve the way I liked him. I wanted to rush out and take the ball from Eve and fling it into the gutter. I wanted to push Quent Younger out of the alley. I wanted to yell, NO. NO. NO.

Eve swung the ball, which hit seven pins, and then she turned and smiled at Quent and they just looked at each other for a minute. Eve's eyes widened and she almost seemed to stop breathing. I knew that was the end of me and Quent. I just knew it.

* * *

I waited every day for something to happen, but it didn't. Things went on just the same. Quent went out with me; Quent went out with Eve. I began to think maybe I'd been wrong. That the looks I saw going between Eve and Quent had just been looks, nothing meaningful. But when I did see Quent, I couldn't relax. I wanted to just come right out and ask him, "Hey, do you *really* like Eve?" But I didn't. I was afraid of the answer.

My mother noticed that I was tenser. "What's going on?" she asked. She may not have noticed white specks on my face, but this she noticed.

"Nothing's going on," I answered. "I don't know what you're talking about."

She shrugged and didn't say anything more. That just made me angrier. She could have pressed, I thought. She could have asked again.

My mood wasn't helped any by the nights I woke up and heard my parents fighting. I was always still half asleep, and I will say for them that they didn't scream at each other. So all I heard were isolated phrases and the tone of their voices. Annoyance. Impatience. Upsetting sounds that made me want to go downstairs and tell them to go out somewhere and have their fights.

Words drifted up the stairs.

". . . why don't you think first?"

". . . too uptight."

". . . they expected us."

". . . can forget."

". . . too often."

I put my hands over my ears and huddled under the covers.

And then the day came. I realized later I'd been waiting for it with so much fear that it was a relief when it actually came.

Eve and I were in her room going through her closet, to see what she didn't want to wear anymore that I wanted to have. There was a pile of things on her bed I was going to try on, when Eve just sank down onto the floor and closed her eyes.

"Okay," I said. "If you don't want me to take this stuff, I won't. You don't have to dramatize."

She opened her eyes and there were tears in them. "Eve, what's wrong?" I asked.

She cried softly, wiping her nose with the back of her hand. "It's Quent," she said.

A surge of happiness absolutely consumed me. He had dumped Eve! Nothing else could make her cry like that. Then a surge of guilt took the place of the happiness. Some friend I was, overjoyed because Quent had dumped

Eve. I patted Eve's shoulder and waited for her to stop crying.

She reached up to her bedside table, grabbed some tissues, and wiped her eyes. "I saw him last night," she said.

I waited.

"Pheb, he told me he really likes me and isn't going to take out any other girls . . . and he wants me just to go out with him, too."

The room was totally silent. I could hear Eve sniffling and my heart beating and Heather moving around in the room next to Eve's. I could smell popcorn and the half-eaten apples on the floor, and the damp fall air coming through a crack in the window. But I felt nothing. Nothing.

Eve reached over and touched my hand. "Phoebe?" she questioned. "Do you mind?"

Then I felt. Did I mind? I hated it. I was angry and confused and I hated Eve, too. But why should I hate Eve? It wasn't her fault. But I did hate her. For her beautiful face and her beautiful sister and her parents who didn't fight.

But when I was finally able to look at Eve . . . she was still Eve. My best friend. My constant companion. My sharer of good and bad. Her eyes were wide and wet and she was waiting for me to say something . . . something.

Did I mind?

"I mind," I said.

Eve was motionless. "Then I won't see him anymore," she said. *"We're* best friends."

I shook my head. "That's dumb. I mean, just because you won't see him doesn't mean he's going to like me. I mean, he might like Scarlett instead."

"Or Melanie," Eve answered.

But it wasn't working. We were trying to be as we had been, but we weren't succeeding.

"What should we do?" Eve asked pitifully.

Why should I be the one who has to decide? I thought. Why put this on me?

"It's not your fault, Eve," I said. I *did* mean it. "You can't help it if he likes you better than any other girl, including me."

"Maybe he likes superficial girls," Eve said, sniffling.

"Maybe all boys do," I answered, thinking of what Heather had said.

"You're too good for him," Eve said.

I knew she meant it, too. This was a part of Eve I didn't understand.

"Quent won't change us, Eve. We're friends, no matter how many boys like you or me, or don't like you or me."

Eve grabbed my hands and held on to

them tightly. "Do you mean it, Pheb? Really? We'll still be best friends?"

"I mean it," I answered. Then I knew I had to go home, right that minute. I picked up my coat and started to the stairs.

"I'll call you tonight," Eve shouted after me.

When I got to the front door I heard steps behind me. It was Heather, racing down the stairs.

"Are you okay?" she asked. "I was listening to every word."

"That's eavesdropping," I said critically. Though I was actually glad she had heard.

"I know," she answered. "I always eavesdrop. It's the way I hear the most important things."

I felt tears in my eyes and turned away from Heather. She put her arms around me and murmured in my ear, "It will be all right, Pheb. You're a super girl. You'll find someone better than Quent. I mean, if he prefers Eve to you, he's nuts."

I laughed. "That's not true, Heather. Eve is . . . special."

She lifted my chin and looked right into my eyes. "So are you, Phoebe. Real special."

I left and walked home slowly. Sure, I thought. Real special. So special Quent Younger didn't want to go out with me anymore.

# Chapter 8

It didn't take long for everyone, I mean everyone, to notice that Quent and Eve were not *just* going out, but were *really* going out. Quent never actually discussed this new arrangement with me. One day he just muttered at me, "Eve told you, didn't she?"

I nodded yes and that was all he ever said to me about it. When I mentioned to Carrie Donovan that it seemed as if he could have done more than mumble at me, she said, "Boys don't like to confront."

"What does 'confront' mean?" I asked.

"You know," she said, "really think about what happened. Examine it. Explain it. Discuss it. At length."

Did I want to confront? I wondered. Did I want to know exactly what Quent Younger preferred about Eve? Was it that her eyes were bigger or her laugh nicer or her hair curly? Was it that she made him feel more like Tarzan than I did, or was she a better Jane? I did want to know, but I also knew I couldn't bear it.

Eve and I tried. We really did. We still talked on the phone every night, but the silences between sentences grew longer. And the images of Eve and Quent walking through the halls at school together, always together, grew sharper.

The night I was going to my first party since Quent had dumped me (that's what he'd done, wasn't it?), I knew what my mother had meant the first day I went to school in Owentown, when she'd said, "Go on, Pheb, the first day is only once."

I was really stupid, I actually waited all day for Eve to call so we could synchronize our clothes, like we'd always done. But by five o'clock, I knew she wasn't going to. What girl who is really going out with a boy wants to look like her best friend?

At dinner, though, I was still hopeful that Eve would call. I pushed the food around on my plate and hardly ate anything. My father asked cheerfully, "Well, Phoebe, any plans for tonight?"

"Lynn Mandel is having a party."

"Nice," my father said. "Are you going with that Quent boy?"

I closed my eyes for a moment and took

a shallow breath. "No. I'm going by myself."

My mother smiled falsely and said in a loud voice. "Walt, that shirt you're wearing is really attractive."

It would have been a nice thing for her to say, and a good way to change the subject, which I knew she was desperately trying to do, except I knew she hated that shirt. My father looked at my mother strangely and then looked down at the shirt. She had never asked me what had happened to Quent, not ever. It had made me angry, but at least I knew now she had noticed. Then *why* hadn't she asked? Did she care so little?

My father knew that Eve and I had both been seeing Quent, so he asked, "Oh, is it Eve's turn tonight?"

I blinked my eyes to clear away the tears that were forming. "Yes, it's Eve's turn tonight," I answered. And every other night, I thought.

Later, as I dressed for Lynn's party, I said to myself, "Go on, Pheb, the first party is only once."

I went through my closet until I found something that had the least memories of Eve attached to it . . . a pale pink sweater and a white skirt. I tied my hair back with a wide white band, something I hadn't done in a long time. As I brushed my hair over the band, I heard loud voices downstairs

. . . laughter . . . and then steps running up the flight of stairs.

Heather appeared in the doorway to my room, her cheeks flushed, her eyes warm. "Hi," she said, as if she always dropped into my bedroom.

"What are you doing here?" I asked her suspiciously.

"I was just driving by and thought I'd come in to say hello," she lied. Her eyes took in the pink sweater and white skirt. "Is that what you're wearing to Lynn's?"

"Yes," I said, still suspicious. Why had she come?

Heather brushed past me and went to the closet. "Don't you think it looks too summery?" She pushed things around in the closet and pulled out a blue jumpsuit and a red sweater. "This is better. Don't you think?"

I understood. "Is Eve wearing white and pink?"

Heather nodded and sat down on the bed. I guess Eve had picked something that had no memories of *me*. That made me feel better somehow.

"Is that why you came over?" I asked. "So I wouldn't be wearing what Eve is wearing?"

"I guess so. It seemed the nice thing to do."

"How did you know?" I asked her. "How

did you know Eve and I wore the same colors? We never told anyone."

Heather smiled. "Phoebe, you used to come to our house after a million parties. It couldn't have been an accident that the two of you were always wearing the same colors in reverse."

I sat down next to Heather. "It's awfully nice of you to do this. Though I still don't understand why you *are* doing it."

Heather smiled, "Well, when I was a kid I had a best friend and we went you and Eve one better. Sometimes we'd buy the exact same clothes, as if we were twins or something. Well, one day we had this awful fight. It was a Thursday, I remember. Then, on Friday night there was a party and we both went, wearing the same sweater and skirt. I was so mad. There I was in the same clothes as this girl I never wanted to speak to again. I don't know . . . I thought of that tonight. And . . . well . . . I wanted to keep you from a rotten night like I had. You're a good kid, Pheb. We women have to stick together. Help each other, you know."

"Heather, Eve didn't do anything bad. It isn't her fault Quent likes her more than me."

Heather shrugged. "I guess. It's just easier to be nice to someone who isn't your sister."

Heather jumped up from the bed. "C'mon,

put your clothes on and I'll drive you over to Lynn's. And smile . . . a lot."

I dreaded walking through the door into Lynn's living room, but I couldn't spend the entire night on her porch, so I closed my eyes and rang the doorbell. The room was crowded when I walked in, and at first I didn't see Eve or Quent. Eve saw me first and came right over.

"You look wonderful," she said. "I always ached after that jumpsuit."

"You look good, too," I said. The white sweater emphasized the darkness of her hair and eyes, and the pink skirt swirled around her legs. Heather had been right.

Quent came over just then and put his hand on Eve's shoulder. "I want to dance," he said. And then, "Hi, Pheb."

He was embarrassed. And I was glad. Let him be. He should be. But then he took Eve's hand and pulled her away. Eve looked at me and smiled awkwardly. "I'll see you later, Pheb."

What was it Carrie had said? Boys don't like to confront? It isn't that they don't like to, I thought. They don't *want* to. They don't know how to be civilized. I had been ready to be charming, friendly, pretend everything was just fine, and he hadn't given me a chance. It wasn't fair.

I wandered into the dining room where there were sodas and chips and nuts and candy. Mrs. Mandel was a big candy lady. Ernie Farber was filling a glass when he saw me. "Want some?" he asked.

Ernie wasn't exactly articulate, but he was kind. "Sure," I answered.

He handed me his glass. "Pepsi, okay?"

I nodded. Then we stood in silence. Say something, I thought. One of us has to say something. But it was Ernie who broke what seemed like a week of lack of communication.

"Listen, Phoebe, I have these tickets for the play the Owentown Players are doing next week. My dad gave them to me. Want to go?"

So Ernie knew, too . . . about Quent and Eve. Nothing like being second fiddle to the world at large.

"I thought you liked Eve," I said, feeling mean.

Ernie shrugged. "I got over her."

"That was fast. You just feel sorry for me. Eve never knew you were alive and Quent doesn't care that I am. We make a perfect couple." I didn't know where the words had come from. It wasn't like me to say things like that, to be that blunt, not caring if I was hurting someone else's feelings besides my own.

But Ernie surprised me. Mild, meek Ernie

held his own. He looked right into my eyes and didn't even blink. "Not true. I always thought you were great, Phoebe. You were always nice to me."

I'm the greatest, I thought. As great as Elizabeth the Great. As great as the Great Wall of China. As great as the Great Train Robbery. I was playing the game Eve and I always played. Only now I was playing it alone.

Ernie was waiting for an answer. "I'd like to go with you, Ernie. I'm sorry I was so mean. What play are they doing?" I asked, hoping it was something funny.

"*Peter Pan*," he replied. Then he grinned. "I know you think it's a baby play, but that's what they're doing."

This is going to be great, I thought. *Peter Pan*.

The rest of the evening was mostly an effort on my part not to keep looking at Eve and Quent. I was never alone for long enough to stare anyway. Mostly because of the girls at the party. They must have formed some kind of pact, because as soon as I was by myself for more than three seconds a girl would come over and talk to me or bring me a sandwich or lead me over to another group. I almost felt like an invalid, but I did like the attention. The boys were like they had always been. I danced with some, joked with some, nothing had changed. Except for Quent. He didn't even ask me to dance once. In fact, he didn't dance with anyone except Eve. When she was dancing with another guy, he either just watched her or talked to the other boys. He was different.

When my father came to pick me up, Eve ran over. "I'll call you tomorrow," she said. How I wished we were leaving together, to spend hours talking about the party and everyone who had been there.

On the drive home, my dad said, "You were the prettiest girl there."

"Dad, you didn't even *see* all the girls there."

I saw him shrug. "I didn't have to. I know you were the prettiest."

It just came out, "Prettier than Eve?"

He turned to me briefly, then back to the road. "Your mother told me about Eve and this Quent person."

Now he was this Quent person. "Oh," I whispered.

We were silent. I had talked about a lot of things with my father. My own personal, gigantic money problems, namely shortage thereof. School problems. Politics. At eight I had been the best shortstop on the block, because my dad had taught me how to play baseball. But never, never had we talked boy-girl things.

Well, it was now or never. "Dad, what makes a boy like one girl more than another?"

"Different things at different times in the boy's life, I guess," he said. "At fourteen, fifteen, a lot of it is chemistry. Or the girl looks good to him. A lot of it is the way the girl makes the boy feel about himself."

He seemed to drift away from me, but he went on. "When I was fourteen, I fell in love with Marcia Yothers. She wasn't even pretty, but she was the smartest girl in our class. And she liked me. I guess I felt if the smartest girl in the class liked me, I must *really* be something."

What did Eve make Quent feel about himself? Or was it mainly chemistry? And if so, what was wrong with *my* chemistry?

As I was getting into bed later, my mother came into the bedroom and sat on the edge of my bed. It's family night, I thought.

"Have a good time?" she asked.

"It was okay."

"Was it okay with Quent and Eve there?"

Boys might not want to confront, but I did. "Mom, why didn't you ever ask me about Quent? You knew he wasn't coming around. You knew I wasn't going out with him."

My mother smoothed out the sheets. "I figured if you wanted to talk to me about it, you would have brought it up yourself. Is that so wrong?"

I didn't know. I had wanted her to ask. But if she had, I probably would have bitten her head off. Maybe mothers couldn't win.

# Chapter 9

Eve kept her word. She called the next morning at nine. She was so prompt that I felt she had written on her appointment calendar, in big red letters, *CALL PHOEBE*.

"Want to go to the mall for lunch and browsing?" she asked.

I was so glad she had called I would have gone to Moscow for lunch and browsing. "Sure," I replied.

"I'll be by at eleven. It's nice out, so let's bike down."

We ate at the Burger Den. I am very conventional when it comes to hamburgers . . . maybe some cheese . . . maybe some bacon, but that's as far as I go. Eve will put anything on her burger that doesn't walk away. I watched with disbelief as she took the hamburger, walked to the salad bar, and proceeded to put half of the salad stuff on her hamburger. When she came to our table and sat down, I looked at the poor beef (I hoped) patty covered with green peppers, mushrooms, carrots, broccoli, onions, and potato salad.

"*That* is the most disgusting thing I've ever seen," I said. "I may throw up."

"It's very healthy," Eve said, as she picked up the hamburger, dropping bits of everything as she did.

"That burger is probably made of ground cement," I said, "and you think it's healthy?"

"Eat," Eve ordered.

After lunch we went to Marie Nicole's to browse. Marie Nicole's stuff, which looks like it comes from Paris, really belongs in any five-and-ten, and we can afford it. Eve didn't look like she was browsing. She headed right for the sweater department and began throwing around the sweaters piled on a table.

"What are you looking for?" I asked.

"Yellow," she answered distractedly.

"But you hate yellow sweaters. You've told me that a million times. Remember the time I wanted to buy that one in New York, and you said — "

"I know," Eve interrupted. "But I've changed my mind."

Obviously Quent liked yellow. It wasn't hard to figure that out, and suddenly he was between us. As visible as if he had really been there. Eve looked at me and she smiled with her mouth but her eyes were sad, knowing.

I walked to another counter and pretended I was carefully examining scarves. "Want to come in the fitting room, while I try this on?" Eve asked, looking down at the yellow fuzzy sweater in her hands.

"I want to look at these scarves," I said quickly. "I *really* need a new one."

I watched Eve walk to the try-on rooms. It was a first for us. The first time, in all the years of shopping together, either one of us had gone into a try-on room without the other. But I just couldn't. I couldn't watch Eve put on the yellow sweater that Quent would look at and think Eve was gorgeous in . . . which she would be.

The rest of the day we roamed from store to store, trying to pretend that the bag with the yellow sweater Eve was carrying didn't exist.

When we got back to my house, Eve got off her bike and hugged me. It was a special hug: tight, almost desperately tight. I hugged her back, just as desperately, seeing over her shoulder the bag from Marie Nicole's stuffed in her bike basket. Suddenly, I realized I hadn't told her about Ernie.

"I forgot to tell you," I said.

"Forgot what?"

"Can you come in for a few minutes?" I asked.

Eve hesitated and took a quick look at her watch. Was Quent coming to her house? Was she meeting him somewhere?

"Sure," Eve said, "but not too long."

We went into the kitchen and I pulled some orange juice out of the refrigerator. "I have a date for Friday night."

Eve's eyes widened and she grinned. "Super. Who with?"

"Ernie Farber," I said, waiting.

"*Ernie Farber*," she yelled. "Oh, Pheb, why?"

I was angry then. First she steals Quent away from me and then she deplores, really deplores, a boy I'm going to go out with.

"He's a *perfectly* nice boy, Eve," I said, my voice quavery and loud.

Eve put down her glass of juice. "I'm sorry, Pheb. Of course, he is. Really. He's . . . unusual. Really."

Unusual. That was a great word to use to describe a boy. King Kong was unusual, so was Jack the Ripper, and so were vampires. I just stared at Eve coldly.

"What are you going to do?" she asked brightly.

Things were going from bad to worse. "We're going to see *Peter Pan*. The Owentown players are doing it," I answered defiantly.

Eve was silent and then she just couldn't help it. She burst out laughing. *"Peter Pan?* Oh, Pheb, you have to admit it's funny . . . *Peter Pan* with Ernie Farber."

I knew she was right. It was funny, but at that moment I didn't want to laugh with Eve about Ernie, so I just said angrily, "I don't see *anything* humorous about it. Not at all."

Eve stopped laughing, and we just looked at each other, hardly recognizing who the other person was. Eve shrugged. "Don't you think Ernie is a little like Frank Kennedy? I mean, he was sort of bumbling and awkward, too. Look, you're getting something Scarlett married."

Good try, Eve, I thought. But it didn't work. "I think he's more like . . . more like. . . ." I was stuck.

"Rhett?" Eve asked, about to burst out laughing again.

The comparison of Rhett Butler and Ernie Farber was too much even for me. I opened my mouth and let the spasms of hysterical laughter out. It was such a relief to be laughing with Eve.

The next day I looked for Eve in the cafeteria at lunchtime. She was sitting at a table for two with Quent. She met my eyes and waved, then she pointed to an empty chair nearby and motioned for me to bring it over to her table. But a table for two is just that . . . a table for two. If it was meant to be for three or four it would have been made for three or four. I shook my head no, smiled broadly, and put my tray on the table Carrie Donovan was sharing with Lynn.

I like Carrie, a lot. She is a small girl with red hair and lots of freckles. She is friendly and open and cute-looking. I decided as I sat down next to her there was no reason why she couldn't be my best friend. After all, she was a perfectly nice girl. So she wasn't Eve. So what? But I knew, nobody had to tell me, you can't just decide someone is going to be a best friend, cut and dried like that. It wasn't the way it worked. A best friend either happened immediately, like Eve and me, or it took time to turn a friend into a best friend. You couldn't push it.

"I have a date with Ernie Farber Friday night," I said. "And we're going to see *Peter Pan.*" Let's get this out and over with, I thought.

Carrie and Lynn exchanged a surprised look and then Lynn said, "Good for you!"

"Why good for me?" I asked.

"Well," Lynn said, "I mean, good that you're not mooning around over Quent

Younger. That you are going to get back on the horse."

"What have horses to do with this?" I asked, completely confused.

"Come on, Phoebe," Carrie said. "You know that when a horse throws you, you're supposed to get up and get right back on, so you won't be scared of riding forever after."

"So?" I asked.

"Don't be dense, Phoebe," Lynn interrupted. "You've been hurt by Quent, but you're not going to let it turn you off boys. You're going out with Ernie and that's good. I admire you for it."

"Me, too," Carrie said. "I admire you, too."

"Really?" I said, feeling as if a huge boulder had been lifted from my back. "You admire me?"

I had been feeling so unworthy, so unlikable just because Quent had rejected me, that having two people who were not either my mother or my father admire me made me take another look at who Phoebe Hadman was. Maybe I wasn't so unappealing after all.

"You don't think Ernie is a wimp?" I asked.

Carrie grinned. "No more wimpy than three quarters of the boys we know. Name one boy you think isn't at least half turkey."

"Eve thinks Ernie is like Frank Kennedy," I said.

Lynn frowned. "What grade is he in? I don't think I know him."

Okay, I thought, so they don't know who Frank Kennedy is. And maybe they've never even heard of Scarlett O'Hara, though that seemed impossible. But they admire me. That's something.

By the time Friday night came I wished I lived in Siberia, or Tashkent, or Peru. Anywhere that Ernie Farber didn't live, so that I wouldn't have to go out with him. I am basically a fair person, so I dressed carefully, wanting to look nice . . . after all, he couldn't help not being Quent. I pulled my hair back into a long braid and wore a new lavender blouse and a short brown skirt. A lot of people would say those colors didn't go together, but they did.

When Ernie picked me up, he stuttered at my mother and father, and I almost stuttered back. Ernie was wearing a *tie*. I mean a real tie.

We took the bus down to the theater and both of us peered out of the windows, as if we were riding past the most fascinating, irresistible streets in the country. But since neither of us had anything to say, the streets were fascinating . . . in comparison.

The play wasn't too bad. And I have to

admit when Tink was dying, and Peter Pan asked everyone who believed in fairies to clap, I was touched.

After the play was over Ernie said, "Would you like something to eat? Or something?"

"Sure," I said, expecting we'd go to Open where all the kids went all the time.

"Okay," Ernie said thoughtfully. "How about Teddy's?"

I knew Teddy's. It was a grown-up-type place. My parents took me there after a movie sometimes. It has lots of plants and classical music. Teddy's was so quiet and dim, none of the kids would be there. There wouldn't be another soul we could talk to, leaving just Ernie and me to carry on what had so far been a tense evening. And then I realized that was why Ernie suggested Teddy's . . . because he knew Eve and Quent wouldn't be there.

As we walked toward the restaurant, I felt a sudden warmth for Ernie. He had been so thoughtful . . . of me . . . of my feelings. That was nice. But when we got to Teddy's and sat down, the quietness of the place washed away the feeling of warmth. How would I get through this? Maybe there would be a sudden fire and we'd all — all five people in the place — have to rush out.

The waitress brought us menus and I opened mine and looked down it. I had to bite my lips to keep from gasping. When you go to a place with your parents you don't look at prices, you just order. When you go with a boy, you look at prices. And these prices were something to look at. It was expensive, at least for Ernie it was expensive.

"We'll split the check," I said. "Since you paid for the play."

"I didn't pay. My dad gave me the tickets. I'm paying for this," he said. But his voice was quavery and he looked pale.

There was a couple my parents' age at the next table. The woman was drinking something out of a tiny, tiny cup. How expensive could anything that tiny be? I thought. It had to be the cheapest thing on the menu.

The waitress came to our table and looked at me inquiringly. "I'll have what that lady is drinking," I said, pointing to the next table.

"You want *that*?" the waitress said with surprise. "You want espresso?"

"Of course," I said firmly, now that I at least knew the name of what I was ordering. "I just love . . . espresso."

She shrugged. Ernie ordered a milk shake which made her shrug again. Ernie and I stared around the empty restaurant and talked in brief phrases about the play, and then the waitress was back. I picked up the tiny cup, took a sip, and almost spit it out right on the table. It was the worst stuff I had ever tasted. I knew it was coffee, but it was strong and bitter and I wanted to cry.

Ernie looked at me. "Is it good?" he asked sceptically.

"Delicious!" I answered with assurance. "It isn't something *everyone* would like. You have to acquire a taste for it. But I just love it. Really."

Ernie reached for my cup. "Can I taste it?"

"Sure," I said, thinking, drink it all, please.

He sipped it and then made a face that made me burst out laughing. "Phoebe, this stuff is *awful*. You can't drink that. Why did you order it?"

"I thought it would be cheap," I said. "Teddy's is so expensive, and I figured a tiny cup like that couldn't cost much. I didn't know it would taste like a laxative."

Ernie pushed the cup away and placed his milk shake in the middle of the table. He pointed one of the straws in my direction. "Come on. We'll share this."

I took a big draw on the straw and almost fainted with delight as the sweet rich liquid flowed into my mouth, removing the espresso taste. Ernie and I looked at each other and we both laughed. Something had happened. Some dam of nervousness and self-consciousness had broken and I felt relaxed. I almost even liked Ernie's tie.

"That was a nice thing you did, Pheb, ordering something cheap."

"I'd hate to be carted off to jail, just because we couldn't pay the bill at Teddy's," I said. "I mean, if I'm going to go to jail it should be for something important."

"Like what?" Ernie asked, looking at me closely.

I had just said words. I hadn't really meant anything serious. Now I had to answer him. What was important to me? I wasn't sure.

"I guess maybe demonstrating against nuclear bombs, or against apartheid . . . things like that. I don't know, Ernie. I haven't thought much about it. Just like I still don't know what I'm going to be someday." I was embarrassed by my lack of maturity. "Do you?" I asked.

"Do I what?" Ernie said.

"Do you know what you're going to be when . . . when you grow up, I guess?"

"I do," Ernie answered. "I'm going to be a writer."

"A writer?" I giggled, and then, feeling like a clod, I put my hand over my mouth. "Sorry. But writers, Ernie, I thought they were supposed to experience all sorts of things. And you . . . well, Ernie, you're very nice, but you hang back. Like at parties, you don't hang around with the kids, you just. . . ."

"Watch," Ernie said, nodding. "I watch. I see a lot of things."

I was interested now. "Like, what do you see?"

Ernie thought. "Well, like how hard some of the kids try to have a good time, like Chuck. Always working at it. And how Eve is scared."

Now I laughed out loud. "Ernie, you are watching your own stories. Eve, scared? You're crazy. What is she scared of?"

"I don't know. I just know she is," Ernie said. "I never said I knew *what* scared her."

I remembered the morning Eve and I had been walking to school and she had said, "I'm sort of strawberry icing . . . but *you* are the cake." I remembered the look that had crossed her face, so quickly gone. She had been scared.

I looked at Ernie with something new . . . respect. He might not mingle much but he was right, he watched. Then I felt nervous; was he watching me? Now? But all he was doing was taking some money out of his wallet to pay the check.

We took the bus home, and in front of my

house I hoped, how I hoped, he wouldn't kiss me. Ernie was nice, but not kissing nice. But he didn't try. He just took my hand and said, "I had a good time, Phoebe. Will you go out with me again sometime?"

"Sure," I replied, and I meant it.

"I won't wear a tie next time."

I blushed in the dark. How had he known I had been put off by the tie? I heard the grin in his voice as he said, "I told you I watch. And your face says just what you're feeling."

Great, I thought. I'm about as mysterious as Donald Duck. But then I thought of Scarlett, as she was in the movie; her face always mirrored what she felt.

# Chapter 10

I was surprised that Eve called the next morning. "How was it?" she asked. Before I could answer she said, "Hey, can you come over for a little while? I want a blow-by-blow."

I was supposed to help my mother take some things to a crafts show in town, but I had to see Eve. She wanted me.

I ran downstairs to my mother's studio, where she was packing bowls in boxes. "Ma, can this wait? I have to go over to Eve's for just a little while." I know I sounded breathless and excited.

My mother stood still, a small ashtray suspended in one hand. I kept telling her not to make ashtrays because it just encouraged smoking, but she never listened to me. "No," she said, "this *can't* wait. Eve can."

"Mom, only for an hour. Please. Eve is

probably busy the rest of the day and she asked me to come over."

"Phoebe," my mother looked like she was about to embark on some kind of in-depth leture, but then she stopped and just seemed thoughtful. "Okay, one hour. Then back here and help me. I can't cart all this stuff alone."

When I got to Eve's she was busy tearing old posters off her walls, and packing up stuffed animals. "What are you doing?" I asked her.

She began smoothing a new bedspread, with a wild abstract print on it, over her blankets. "It's time for a new look in this room. Something more sophisticated, more meaningful."

I picked up a stuffed frog and held it to me. "I like the way the room looked."

"You can have the frog," she said. "I don't really want it anymore."

I rubbed my nose against the soft green of the frog's back and said, "Thanks. I'd like it. But Eve, I never knew you liked this kind of modern art stuff." I gestured toward her new bedspread.

Eve looked at the spread, too. "Well . . . I'm developing a taste for it. Quent says my room should be more *now*."

"Oh," I answered, not sure what he meant by that. I had always felt very *now* in Eve's room, very aware of what was going on every minute.

Eve sank down on the bed and pulled me with her. "So how was last night?"

I saw Ernie sitting opposite me, pushing his milk shake toward me. "Ernie is a nice guy. Sweet, kind of. Thoughtful. And the play isn't really that babyish, at least not all of it."

Eve grabbed her hairbrush off the table next to her bed and started brushing. It suddenly occurred to me that whenever Eve didn't know what else to do she brushed her hair. "Sweet boys are bor — ing. No real excitement in them. Ashley was really sweet and you have to admit he couldn't hold a candle to Rhett."

I straightened up. "And since Melanie loved Ashley and you thought *she* was boring, that must make me boring, too, because I think Ernie is sweet." My voice shook with anger.

Eve's eyes grew wide and she got a little paler. "I didn't say that, Phoebe. I don't think you're boring at all."

I stood up and shouted at her. "I suppose you think you and Quent are Scarlett and Rhett. Oh-so-wild-and-wonderful a couple."

Eve stood up, too, and reached over to touch me, but I backed away. "I didn't say that, either, Pheb. I didn't at all."

"No, but that's what you meant. You said I was a frightened rabbit."

"When you were in *second grade!*" Eve was shouting, too.

"Well, I wasn't," I yelled. "Not ever!" I ran out of her room and down the stairs. My bike was leaning against a tree and I grabbed it and pedaled away as fast as I could, tears stinging my eyes.

I could hear Eve, who was now outside her house, yelling after me, "Phoebe, wait!"

That night I thought about the morning a lot. Eve was right, she hadn't said anything like what I had accused her of. It had all been me. I had to be honest; I couldn't stand Eve and Quent being a couple. Eve had it all. Quent, parents who didn't fight, and even a sister like Heather. And what did I have? Ernie Farber?

I called Eve in the morning. "I'm sorry," I said. "I was dumb. You really didn't say anything mean to me at all."

Eve's voice was low and sad. "I'm glad you called, Pheb. I didn't mean to hurt your feelings. Really, I didn't."

"I know. Look, Eve, I'll see you in school. Okay?"

"Okay," she said. There was a pause while both of us hung onto the phone. Neither of us wanting to be the first to hang up. Then I put down the receiver.

We saw each other at school, and once in a while we ate lunch together, once in a while we'd talk on the phone. But not too often. And when we did it was stiff, hard to talk to each other . . . but we kept trying. But finally there were two weeks when we didn't see each other, except for English class. And we didn't talk on the phone, either.

And then one Saturday afternoon I was Christmas shopping at Udall's Department Store and I saw Eve. I had been trying to decide whether to buy her a Christmas present or not, and if I bought her one what to get her. She looked up as I was staring at her and the Eve smile lit up her face. I smiled back and waved frantically. She dropped the nightgown she had in her hands and ran, really ran, over to me. And in the middle of the store we hugged.

She grabbed my hand and started pulling me along with her. "What are you looking for?"

"Something for my mother and father. I don't have the foggiest."

"You could buy your mother some clay," she said.

"Or cinnamon," I answered.

"Or an ironing board," Eve countered.

We laughed and hugged again. Nothing had changed, I told myself. Look at us, just like we were.

We shopped that day, and ate at Open, and giggled about everyone who came in. When we picked up our packages to leave, I pointed to a box Eve was carrying. "What's in that?"

Eve looked away. "It's just a present."

I nodded. For Quent, of course. Lots had changed, but could I blame Eve for it? I wished I could. I wanted to.

I went back to Udall's the next day and bought Eve a gold clip for her hair. I could see it shining in the dark curls.

On Christmas day I rode over to the Patterson's and shyly gave Eve the box. She picked up a package from under the tree and handed it to me. In it was a tortoiseshell band for my hair. I put it on and the rich brown looked elegant in my blonde hair.

"How about that?" Eve said. "We both bought hair stuff."

"Funny," I said.

Eve grabbed my hand and started pulling, just like always. "Come upstairs and let me show you some of the stuff I got."

We had turned to the staircase when the bell rang. Quent stood on the doormat holding a small box. He held it out to Eve and she pulled him in. Eve just couldn't resist pulling.

Quent smiled at me. A small smile, an awkward smile. Eve was tearing the paper off the box Quent had given her. She gasped as she opened it and held up the most delicate gold chain from which hung a small gold heart. It was so beautiful . . . and so romantic.

Then she gave him a box. There was a big, antique horn in it, to attach to his bike. "Hey," he yelled. "How about that?"

Then they oohed over their presents some more and looked at each other with . . . what? Love? Like? Whatever it was, I had been forgotten. I left the house quietly. And they never really noticed. I couldn't blame them for not noticing. I mean, if I had just gotten a gold heart on a chain, I wouldn't know who was going in and out of my house, either.

When I got home Ernie was waiting for me . . . with a present. My heart sank. I hadn't even *thought* about buying him anything. But why should I have? We weren't really anything to each other. Maybe friends . . . maybe not even that. I didn't know.

My mother and father left the room and Ernie thrust his package at me. I opened it carefully, trying not to rip the nice paper. In it was a book. A book. Poetry by Emily Dickinson. I just stared at it.

Ernie was watching me very carefully. "You think it's a wimpy present. Don't you?"

"No," I said quickly. "No, I don't. I just never have read much poetry." All I could see was the little gold heart Eve had gotten.

"You'll like Dickinson," Ernie said. "I know it."

"I'm sure I will," I said weakly.

Ernie shuffled his feet and then said, "I'd better go. I'll see you in school."

He started to the door and I yelled after him, "Ernie! I'm sorry. I mean, I don't have anything for you. I just. . . ."

"It's okay, Phoebe. I didn't think you'd have anything for me. That's not why I brought you the book."

He left and I felt so ridiculous. I wished I understood him, but I really didn't. He just was a puzzle to me. I wandered into the kitchen where my mother was trying to stuff a turkey, but more of the stuffing was landing on the table than in the turkey.

I still had the book in my hands and my mother said with excitement, "Emily Dickinson! How wonderful! Did Ernie give it to you?"

I nodded. "Eve got a gold heart from Quent," I said, unable to keep the yearning out of my voice.

My mother wiped her stuffing hands on her jeans. "Don't be a jerk, Phoebe. Any boy in this world can give any girl in this world a gold heart. But very few boys would give very few girls Emily Dickinson's poems. Don't you know that?"

I didn't know that. But up in my room I thought about it.

Eve called the next morning, sounding sleepy and confused. "What happened yesterday, Phoebe? One minute you were there and the next you were gone."

I hesitated. "Well, you were sort of busy . . . with your present and Quent and all."

"But you could have at least said good-bye."

"I guess. Sorry. I should have." I thought about whether I should tell her about my present. And then I couldn't resist, no matter what she thought of it. I wanted her to know some boy had given me a present.

"Ernie was here when I got back. He had a present for me, too."

"What was it?" Eve asked with obvious interest.

I hesitated again. Here goes, I thought. "He gave me a book of Emily Dickinson's poetry."

Eve was silent. "Really? A book of poetry? I don't think any boy will ever give me poetry."

There was a wistfulness in her voice that surprised me. But then it was gone. "Listen,

Pheb. I've got to go. Mom wants me to usher in the theater today. One of her people is sick."

I didn't talk to Eve again over the Christmas vacation. Normally we would have been together constantly, but not this year. I saw her around . . . at the mall, at the movies and we'd wave, but she was always with Quent.

The pattern was set . . . or unset. It wasn't her fault. It wasn't mine. It just was. By the time school had started again, we just weren't calling each other anymore. Once or twice I had my hand on the telephone to call her number, but then I just didn't.

At school, outside of being together in English, we had no other classes together. We'd pass in the halls and wave at each other wildly. We'd even stop to talk and we'd both babble at the same time.

"I meant to call, but you know, what with one thing and another."

"We have to meet after school and study."

"I saw you in that new blue skirt yesterday. You looked absolutely gorgeous."

"Listen, call me, or I'll call you next week."

"Sure."

"Sure."

I missed her. I don't know if she missed me. She had Quent. I got friendly with Carrie and Lynn. They were some things Eve wasn't. They were not a lot of things Eve was. But there was no way to really compare them. I missed Eve.

One night at a school basketball game, I saw her across the gym. Not only was she with Quent, but they were sitting with the couples. It was like that. A part of the gym, a part of the cafeteria, a part of the whole school was for the couples. The rest of everything was for the rest of the world . . . the kids who weren't going out with any one person or even going out at all.

Eve didn't see me, but I watched her. Quent had his arm around her shoulders and she was laughing. When our team scored a basket, they both stood up and hugged each other and jumped up and down. I had never felt so outside in my whole life. It wasn't even a matter of just missing Eve anymore, or just wanting Quent to like me. It was my whole social life that was a bore.

Ernie was sitting next to me. Ernie was always sitting next to me. It's funny he could do it in a non-wimpy way. He was just there. He wasn't even asking for anything. I didn't know what we were. Certainly not a couple.

"Pheb," he said, "the game is on the court, not up there." He nodded toward the couples' area.

"I'm not so sure," I said wistfully.

That night in bed, I hated Eve. She was dumb, I thought; all that jumping around and hugging because of a stupid basket. Such immaturity. I fell asleep and then I woke up to the voices, the loud voices, the angry tones. I hated my parents, too. Not tonight, I thought. Not on top of Eve and Quent. I tried not to listen. My door was open a little and I got up to close the fight out, and I couldn't help hearing.

"They're stupid," my mother was yelling. "It's their loss. A wonderful man like you and they just pass over you. They don't know how lucky they are to have someone so superior."

I stopped at the door, confused, and I stood there.

My father's voice was shaky, almost tearful. "I wanted that promotion, so much, Betty. I wanted it for the work, for the prestige, and so much for the money."

"We're doing all right," my mother said. "We manage."

"But Phoebe will be ready for college soon. I wanted to send her to the best."

My mother's voice was firm and strong. "I can get a job. Bea Frank asked me if I'd sell in her gift shop. I can do that."

"But your pottery. You really like doing that and you're good, too."

She was? I thought.

I leaned against my door and kept listening. I knew it was a sneaky thing to do but I couldn't leave.

"I can do both," my mother said. "I can do the pottery at night. I'm a good salesperson, too. Bea will be lucky to get me."

"But Phoebe. I wanted Yale for her or Smith or something wonderful."

There was a rattling of dishes, as if they had been having coffee or something. "Phoebe is strong," my mother said. "She's a survivor. She's got guts. It doesn't matter if she goes to Yale or a college not so fancy, she'll do fine. She's a realist . . . and she loves you."

I closed the door to my room and went back to bed. I couldn't deal with any more than I had heard. They like each other, I thought with amazement. All that fighting and arguing and they really like each other. No one could have heard what they'd been saying to each other and not know that.

But more than what they felt about each other, what my mother had said about me staggered me. I was a survivor? I had guts? How had she come to that conclusion? And what did that mean to me? It made me nervous. Did they think I could take care of myself without much help? Did they think I was a grown-up, ready to take on the world?

I'm just a kid, I thought, and my mother is yelling about me being a survivor. But something about it also made me feel good.

In the morning, they were both at the breakfast table when I came downstairs. My father was buttering a very burned English muffin and dark crumbs were flying onto the table.

"Walt," my mother said with annoyance, "the whole room is going to be filled with your crumbs."

"I'll sweep them up," he answered.

"You never sweep anything up," she complained.

"Well, that makes two of us," he grumbled.

I heard all the usual bickering, but I saw things I hadn't noticed before. Like, he poured her what was left of the coffee and kept the bottom dregsy stuff for himself. And she pushed a jar of his favorite jam toward him. When he left he touched the top of her head with his hand, lightly. No kiss, just the touch, and she tilted her head toward him. That was all.

When he was gone I just stared at my Nutri-Grain. "You really love each other, don't you?" I asked.

My mother looked at me with astonishment. "What a dumb question. Of course, we love each other."

"So why do you fight all the time?" I asked.

"Fight?" she repeated. "When do we fight?"

"All the time. You never agree on anything, like with the crumbs just now."

My mother just stared at me. "That's not fighting, that's just . . . just. . . ."

"Just what?"

My mother looked embarrassed, but I stood firm. I wanted an answer.

"Well," she said, clearing her throat, "sometimes people find it hard to show what they really feel. So they cover up the love they feel with silly arguments. It somehow makes them more comfortable. You'd need a psychiatrist to tell you why. Your father is like that, too, except with you. With you all the love he feels shows. Your father and I, with each other, we just sort of box around, but Phoebe, we do love each other."

"It seems dumb to me. I mean, if you are married and love one another, you should just let it all hang out," I said.

My mother laughed. Then she stopped laughing and grabbed my hand. "I haven't been a good example to you, Pheb. I mean, if you love someone, a friend, a relative, a husband someday, maybe, tell them. Don't keep it a secret. Everyone likes to know that they are loved."

I started to walk to the door when she called after me, "Have you really been thinking that your dad and I don't love each other?"

I nodded. And then I went back to her and I said, "I was listening last night. What did you mean that I was a survivor?"

"You're strong. Look at this Eve-Quent thing. You haven't let it mess you up too much. You've made new girl friends. You go out with Ernie. I know you're not wild about him, but you do things together."

I'm in this so I might as well go all the way, I thought. "How come you know that kind of stuff about me, when you never seem to notice much? Not what I'm wearing, or how I look, or anything."

"You think I don't notice? I notice everything!" she shouted. "I know that right now there is a button off your new white blouse. And there's been a skirt balled up on the floor of your closet for a week. And your hair needs cutting."

"So how come you never say anything?" I shouted back.

She stood up and walked over to me. "I'm giving you room, Phoebe. I'm trying to let you grow up and be a person. My mother was always after me, about everything. My friends, my hair, my clothes, every breath I took. I would have loved a mother like me and you don't want one. You just can't win."

I stood up next to her. "I'm going to be late for school. I have to go. I left my scarf upstairs, I'll go get it."

I ran up to my room and opened my closet door. I pulled out the new white blouse and saw where the missing button should have been. It wasn't even that noticeable, since it was the next to the last button. Then I peered into the bottom of the closet and pulled out my red skirt which was in a ball toward the back. I had been looking for it for a week. Finally, I looked into the mirror and pushed my hair, which needed to be cut, away from my face.

I went back downstairs and into the kitchen. Mother was still at the table, reading the paper and drinking coffee. "I have to think about all this. I'm confused," I said.

But I kissed her before I left and she held me tight. I stood for a minute behind her chair and said, "You were right. There's a button missing from my white blouse."

"I think there's a button missing from your head," she said, but it didn't sound mean.

# Chapter 11

In school, Eve was going out of the ladies' room as I was going in. She waved and smiled and I wanted to grab hold of her and tell her about the night before. Everything I had heard. But I knew it wouldn't satisfy the need I had to talk to someone close to me.

I ate with Lynn and Carrie and I thought about talking to them. But I couldn't. They barely knew my parents, anyway. But it wasn't just that; they just weren't the right ones.

After school, Ernie was waiting for me. He did that a lot. We walked home together, or if it was raining we took the bus. We walked in silence for a little while and then hardly without thinking I asked, "What do you think of my parents?"

"I don't think about them at all," Ernie said.

"I don't mean that way. I mean, how do you think they are with each other?" I persisted.

Ernie thought and then answered. "They like each other."

"How do you know that?"

This time Ernie didn't hesitate. "Remember that night last week I had dinner at your house? Well, we had steak. Remember? And I saw you father look at what he had sliced and then give your mother the best pieces."

"So?" I said, getting a little annoyed at his confusing — to me — answer.

"Well," Ernie said, "steak is very expensive. And you wouldn't give the best pieces to someone you didn't like."

"I don't know," I said. "That seems awfully simple."

We walked in silence a little further, and then I said, "If someone said to you, 'Phoebe is a survivor,' what would that mean?"

Ernie stopped walking and looked at me. "You mean, like after a flood or an earthquake or something?"

"No," I said with irritation. "I mean in just an ordinary day in Owentown."

"I guess it means you cope or something. You know, one of the reasons I don't spend every weekend with my father, like the custody agreement my parents have says, is because the least little thing that goes wrong he gets a headache. My mother, on the other hand, well, she just does what has to be done."

I thought about what Ernie had said. And suddenly I knew what Ernie and I were . . . we were friends. Not like Eve and me, because I could never talk clothes and makeup and stuff like that with him, but we were friends anyway.

When we reached my door I said, "Want to come in?"

I usually don't do that and Ernie smiled broadly. "I can't today. I have to study for that French test. Tomorrow?"

"Sure."

The weeks went by. I got used to being without Eve. That didn't mean I didn't still miss her, but it didn't hurt like it had in the beginning. I even got used to seeing her with Quent. I didn't like them as a couple, but I didn't want to wail every time I saw them. Then I got so used to seeing them together, that I didn't really notice them anymore. Well, almost didn't notice. I even got used to my parents' bickering. When I'd wake up in the middle of the night and hear them arguing about something, I'd just roll over and think, Oh, grow up.

The weeks went by and I was together again, or as together as I had been before

Quent and I and Eve and I had broken up. On a Monday, I went into the cafeteria at lunchtime, looking for Carrie. She wasn't there yet, so I sat at a table and read while I waited for her. After a few minutes I looked around the room and I saw Eve. She was alone at a table. She looked awful. Her hair needed to be washed, her face was blotchy, and her eyes were red and swollen. She just sat there and pushed a carton of milk around the table. Then she stopped pushing and just gazed across the cafeteria, her face collapsing into the most heartbreaking look of pain. I turned to see what she was gazing at. There was Quent Younger. He was walking in with his arm around a small, red-haired girl. She was looking up at him, laughing and flirting, subtly but obviously. Quent was returning the flirting looks, only he wasn't as good at it.

Eve just stared. With a grunt of disgust, I got up and walked over to Eve's table. I began gathering Eve's books together. "Come on," I said.

Eve looked at me dumbly. "Come on where?" she asked, her eyes filling with tears.

"Well, you're not going to just *sit* there and *stare* at them, are you?" I asked.

"I don't know where else to stare," Eve said, sniffling loudly.

"Eve, we're leaving. Now. We'll get our coats and leave school."

"That's cutting," Eve said. "I've never done that."

"Neither have I," I replied. "But you can't just sit here and let him see you looking like such a mess."

I took another look at Quent who was now sitting with the girl, and he was just as entranced by Miss Nameless as he had been with Eve. He certainly didn't hang around long with any one person. Maybe Eve hadn't been enough Jane, either.

I tugged at Eve's arm and she got up docilely. I pulled her out of the cafeteria. Funny, now I was the one dragging and tugging. We stopped at our lockers and got our coats and I continued pulling Eve toward the bus.

On the bus, Eve said, "I don't know what happened. One day we were okay and the next he was taking Yolanda out."

"Yolanda?" I said.

"The girl. The redhead. Her name is Yolanda."

My mother was in her studio when Eve and I came into the house. She heard the door slam and came running into the foyer yelling, "Who's there?"

When she saw us she collapsed against the wall. "You scared the life out of me. I thought we were being burglarized or something."

"Pretty noisy burglars," I said.

My mother stood away from the wall and looked at Eve and me. "What's going on? Why are you both here and not at school?"

Eve and I exchanged a frantic look, but it was obvious Eve wasn't going to come up with any useful explanation. She just looked pathetic. "Eve doesn't feel well," I said. That wasn't a lie.

Mother peered at Eve suspiciously. "Why didn't you go to the infirmary?" she asked.

Eve didn't even bother answering. She just started to cry . . . again.

Finally I decided the truth was the best thing. "Quent dumped her. She feels terrible and I brought her home."

A mother is a mother. I saw the fleeting look that crossed my mother's face. Satisfaction. There was no doubt about it, it was satisfaction. But she quickly replaced it with one of sympathy. "What a shame," she said. But I knew she didn't mean it.

"Okay. You can stay here. But don't you ever do anything like this again. Understand?"

We both nodded our heads.

"I'll call school and tell them you're here."

Eve and I went upstairs and Eve just

threw herself on the extra bed. I sat on mine and just looked at her. I may be abnormal or something, but I felt sorry for her. All the Eve energy and excitement were gone. In its place was an unhappy girl. And that girl was Eve, who had been my best friend.

"I feel so embarrassed. All the kids at school know. They sort of stare at me with pity. Even Heather feels sorry for me," Eve said.

"They won't even notice you in a couple of weeks," I said wisely.

"Are you sure?" she asked.

"Sure."

Eve sat up and wiped her nose with the back of her hand. "I see you with Ernie Farber a lot. Do you like him?"

I nodded. "I like him a lot, but as a friend. Not a boyfriend, just as a friend who is a boy."

"No boy like Ernie would ever *look* at me," Eve said softly.

I thought I hadn't heard right and looked for some hidden putdown in the words. But I couldn't find any. "What do you mean?" I asked.

Eve shrugged. "He's so smart. I don't understand half of what he says. When he says something, that is. And he always seems to be, well, watching."

"He wants to be a writer," I said. "That's why he watches."

Eve looked down at her hands. "No boy who wants to be a writer would like me. I'm not serious enough. I always knew you were different."

I went over and sat down next to Eve. "You're crazy, Eve. Any boy would like you. Look at what happened; Quent picked *you*."

"Not for long," Eve said and smiled faintly.

There was a knock at the door and my mother shouted, "Open up!"

She stood there with a tray holding two cups of steaming cocoa and a plate of cookies. Each cup had a huge marshmallow floating on top, slowly melting into the rich chocolate.

"I thought this might cheer you up," she said.

I took the tray and smiled at her. "Thanks." She smiled back and said, "Life is full of surprises, isn't it, Phoebe?"

We drank the cocoa in silence. Then Eve said, "Now I know how Scarlett felt, when she ran home after Melanie died and Rhett told her he was leaving her."

"Yeah, but she also decided to go home to Tara and she said, 'After all, tomorrow is another day.' "

Eve got up and took her hairbrush out of her bag and started brushing her hair. "Yes, but my house is nothing like Tara, and tomorrow I have a dentist appointment."

Eve stopped brushing and looked at me. "I've missed you, Phoebe. Lots."

"I missed you, too, Eve."

Eve started sniffling again. "I felt so awful."

"It wasn't your fault, Eve."

Eve smiled. Not the Eve smile, but not a pathetic one, either. "Are we best friends again?" she asked eagerly.

I was startled. I wasn't ready for this. "Well," I answered, "we're friends anyway."

I saw the look. The frightened one. The one I didn't want to believe was possible. I wanted to do something nice for her, just to make the look go away.

It just came to me. "Eve, listen. You know what you said before, that no boy like Ernie would ever look at you?"

Eve nodded. "It's true. I'm not smart enough."

I began to walk around the room. "Supposing I ask Ernie to get a friend of his, a real smart one, and the four of us will go out together. We'll have a good time. That will prove to you that you're no dummy."

"I didn't say I was a dummy," Eve said, sounding a little like the old Eve. "I said I wasn't smart enough for a smart boy."

"Okay! Okay! But won't it make you feel better if you're wrong?"

"I guess," Eve said. "But what if I'm right?"

"Listen, Ashley was a lot smarter than Scarlett in some ways and he still thought she was beautiful and exciting."

Eve grinned. "But he married *Melanie*."

We sat in silence for a while, but it was a nice silence. Comfortable, warm.

Then Eve asked, "What happened to us, Pheb? Why did we let one stupid boy *tear* us apart?" She let her voice rise as she became more dramatic. Yet I knew she meant what she was saying.

I shrugged. "I don't know. I just always felt so jealous of you. And whenever we were together all I could think of was that Quent liked you better than me."

"And I always felt so guilty," Eve said. "I knew I hadn't done anything wrong, but I *felt* as if I had."

Eve got up and walked around the room. She picked up the stuffed frog she had given me and held it to her. "Could it happen again, Phoebe? Could some other dumb boy come between us?"

"I don't know," I said.

Eve looked teary again. She picked up her coat and said, "I'd better get home." She stood in the doorway and just looked at me.

I ran over to her and we hugged, holding each other tightly. Then she started down the stairs. The frog was on the floor where she had dropped it and I picked him up and ran after her. "Eve, do you want him back?"

She shook her head. "No. I'd like you to have him."

I clutched him to me and called after her, "I'll call Ernie, and we'll set up a date with some brain."

Eve looked up at me. "I think I may regret this."

I went back to my room and turned off the lights and just sat looking out the window. I sat for a long time. It was beginning to snow, large, lacy white flakes that stuck to the bare tree branches. It felt good being with Eve, but it felt different. And I didn't know why different. Not really.

The next afternoon, Ernie was waiting for me after school. As we walked home, I tried to figure out how best to talk to him about a date for Eve. Finally, I just said, "How would you like to double date with someone?"

Ernie was no dope. "Who?" he asked bluntly.

"Well," I said, "I'd like you to ask one of

your smartest friends to go out with you and me and Eve."

Ernie stopped walking and looked at me. "Why with Eve?"

I stopped walking, too. "Because she feels she wouldn't be interesting to a smart boy and I want to prove to her she's wrong."

"Why?" he asked again.

"Ernie," I said with annoyance, "what is this, some kind of third degree?"

"Phoebe, you are asking me to fix up one of my friends. I have a right to know why."

I punched his arm lightly. "I'm not asking you to get a date for the bride of Frankenstein. It's Eve. She's pretty and fun and we'll all have a good time, and — "

"Okay. Okay," Ernie said. "What about Marc Iter?"

I hesitated. "Don't you have anyone a little better-looking?"

"Pheb!" His voice was rising. "What kind of sexist thing is that to say? If a guy said it about a girl — "

"Okay. Marc is fine. Call him. Let's do it Friday night."

Ernie called me later that night and said it was all set, and I called Eve.

"I don't know, Phoebe," she said.

I had never heard Eve so unsure of herself.

"Don't be a jerk, Eve. It's all organized. You're going."

We went to the movies Friday night. Marc was like Ernie used to be, sort of shy, so a movie was a good choice. It was a really super movie, too. It was about this girl whose father commits a crime, nothing awful like murder, he just embezzles some money. I know that isn't a nice thing to do, but nobody died. Anyway, the father goes off to jail and the girl is so ashamed and embarrassed and angry at him that she refuses to have anything to do with him. She won't visit him in prison, won't write to him, won't even talk to anyone about him. Of course her father, who is basically a nice guy and only stole to give his family luxuries (he said), is heartbroken and the girl's mother is heartbroken, too.

After the movie we went to Open and we started to talk about how we'd feel if our fathers were off in jail, and what we would do. It was a good discussion and we were all gabbing away, but Eve wasn't talking about it the way we were.

Eve just joked.

She ran her hand through those dark curls of hers and said, "My father is in his theater so much he might as well be in jail. Who would notice?" She grinned the Eve grin.

I tried to keep the conversation going. "I

think I'd love him anyway, my father, that is. I'd *have* to go to see him, because I'd miss him so much. Eve, come on, what would you really feel?"

"Yeah, Eve. What?" Marc asked. The question didn't sound exactly brilliant, but Marc was trying, too.

Eve laughed again and turned to me. "You know, Pheb, I'm a gypsy, stolen from the gypsy band, so my father isn't even my real father. So I'd just go find the gypsies and ride off in a red wagon with them."

Everyone *did* smile at her. She *was* funny. But then we kept talking, and Eve, well, Eve was restless. She looked around the restaurant, waving at people she knew. She whispered in my ear about the terrible blouse Norma Marks had on. I had to admit she was right, but I wanted to hear what Ernie was saying. Once Eve went to the ladies' room and on her way back to our table she stopped and talked to about five different kids. Once she spilled her Coke and we all had to stop and mop everything up.

And then we went home. Marc was old enough to drive, so he dropped Ernie and me at my house and then he took Eve home.

"So?" Ernie asked.

"So?" I repeated.

"Pheb, how do you think it went?"

"Awful," I said. "It went awful. I don't

want to talk about it anymore, Ernie. Okay?"

Ernie shrugged. "Okay. Okay." He started to walk away from me and then he turned back. "It's no big deal, Phoebe."

Inside, my mother was in the living room reading. I wished she wasn't there. Why couldn't she be potting in her studio?

"So?" she asked.

I was mad. "Can't anyone talk in more than one syllable?"

"Okay, so . . . how . . . was . . . the . . . evening?"

"It could have been better," I said. "Eve didn't have a very good time, I don't think. And because Eve wasn't having a good time, I wasn't having a good time."

My mother closed her book and cleared her throat. I knew what that meant.

"Phoebe, have you ever heard of a writer named Thomas Wolfe?"

"No," I said, "I never did. Does that make me an illiterate?"

"No," she answered. "Let's try again. Did you ever hear of a book called *You Can't Go Home Again?*"

"No," I said belligerently, feeling dumb. "Mom, what are you trying to say, or is this just a pop quiz?"

My mother folded her hands in her lap and then looked at me. "Okay. This writer Wolfe wrote a book called *You Can't Go Home*

*Again.* Does that title mean anything to you?"

"No," I said, still belligerent.

My mother just ignored the tone and said, "It means, Phoebe, that sometimes you can't go back. That what you think you are going back to isn't always there anymore."

"I assume," I said as haughtily as I could, "that you are talking about Eve and me."

"Right," Mother said.

"Well, *I* don't want to talk about Eve and me." I turned to the stairs and felt tears in my eyes.

I didn't sleep very well that night. I kept thinking, you can't go home again; you can't go home again.

In the morning I lay in bed. I saw Eve joking and waving, and spilling her Coke, and talking with half the kids in Open and whispering in my ear. Eve hadn't changed, not a smidgen. She was still Eve, doing all the Eve things. She was there to go home to. So what was different? Easy answer. *I* was different. I wasn't sure how, but I knew I was. Maybe it was that being with Ernie so much had made me more interested in other things. Maybe it was that I didn't need Eve anymore, for practically survival. But it wasn't Eve's fault that *I* had changed.

When the phone rang, I knew it would be Eve.

"I was a dud," she said pitifully.

"You weren't, Eve. You were fine."

"I have the attention span of a three-year-old," she persisted.

"You just like less talk and more action," I persisted.

"A *lot* less talk," she said.

"What did Marc say when he took you home?" I asked, hoping for the best.

"He said, 'I'll see you around.' You know what that is?"

"No, I don't." But I did.

"That, Phoebe, as you well know, is the kiss of death. That means he doesn't really want to see me anywhere except around."

We were silent and then she asked, "Want to go to the mall tomorrow?"

This was hard. "Ernie is coming over and we're going to study for the history exam."

"Okay," Eve said. "I'll see you in school."

"Sure." I hung up.

I sat silently for a long time.

I saw Eve as she probably was right now, sitting on her bed brushing her hair. Then from way back I saw the little hand pushing the tuna fish sandwich toward me. I saw her writing my will, and I heard her saying "You, Phoebe, are a wonderful human being."

Eve was my *friend*. I wanted her to be. But I wanted it *all*. Eve and Ernie and Carrie and the different me. And why not? Who said everything had to stay the same or it couldn't be at all?

Eve would always be Eve and who knew what I'd be? But she was there right now! I knew things wouldn't be *just* the same. But I didn't want them *just* the same.

I threw on jeans and a sweater, ran downstairs, grabbed a glass of orange juice, and biked over to Eve's house. Heather just stared as I ran up the stairs. Eve was sitting on her bed and she had this white stuff in a streak in the center of her head.

When I came into the room she smiled. The Eve smile. The room almost exploded into brilliance.

"What are you *doing*?" I asked.

"I'm putting a gold streak in my hair. See, this white glop takes the color out of my hair. Then I wash out the white and put in the blonde."

"Supposing it looks awful?" I asked. Some things never change about people.

Eve shrugged. "So then I guess I'll put the dark back in. Or something."

I sat on the floor next to Eve's bed. All the stuffed animals were out again and I picked one up that had fallen onto the floor. "Want to go to the mall after you finish that thing?" I nodded my head in the direction of her head.

Eve paused and looked at me with such hope and shyness. "Sure! You want to?"

"Yes. I have to find a new skirt; my red one is so wrinkled it will never look good again."

"That's 'cause you leave things on the floor in your closet all the time," she said knowingly.

She knew so much about me. And I knew as much about her.

She took the timer off her night table and looked at it. Then she said, "Do you think Scarlett talked to her beaux about politics, or the war, or who was president, or what she'd do if she lost Tara?" Eve was serious.

I thought about it. "I doubt it," I said. "That wouldn't be Scarlett."

Eve looked relieved.

"I wish I was more like you," she said, "in some ways, anyway. But I'm me and you're you and I'm just not very deep, I guess."

Then the timer went off. "Hurry," she said, "you can help me."

We pushed each other toward the bathroom and Eve stuck her head in the sink. She grabbed a glass and started filling it with water and pouring it over her head to get the white stuff out. I shouted over the running water and Eve's gasps. "Why don't you just get into the shower and wash the junk out?"

Eve lifted her head. Now the water was dripping all over her sweater and jeans.

She reached over and turned on the shower and then, with all her clothes on, got in. She put her head under the spray, keeping her eyes tightly closed, yelling, and laughing. When the bleach was out of her hair, she held her face up to the water and shook her head wildly.

Suddenly, without thinking, I got into the shower, too. We splashed each other and laughed and I squooshed my feet in my soaking sneakers.

Ernie wouldn't understand this, and Carrie probably wouldn't, either. But I did. And Eve did.

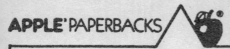